# switchers

## kate thompson

**HYPERION PAPERBACKS FOR CHILDREN**

**New York**

First Hyperion Paperback edition 1999

First Edition
3  5  7  9  10  8  6  4

This book is set in 14-point Perpetua.
Designed by Mara VanFleet.

Library of Congress Cataloging-in-Publication Data
Thompson, Kate.
Switchers/Kate Thompson—1st ed.
p. cm.
Summary: When freakish weather grips the Arctic regions and moves southward,
an Irish girl and her strange companion save the world from disaster through
their ability to switch into animal forms.

ISBN 0-7868-0380-0—ISBN 0-7868-2328-3 (lib. bdg.)
ISBN 0-7868-1396-2 (pbk.)

[1. Weather—Fiction. 2. Imagination—Fiction. 3. Arctic Regions—Fiction. 4.
Animals—Fiction. 5. Dublin (Ireland)—Fiction. 6. Ireland—Fiction.] I. Title.
PZ7.T3715965Sw 1998
[Fic]—21    97-33056

# switchers

ǝ u o   ɹ ǝ ʇ d ɐ ɥ ɔ

The bus seemed to take hours to crawl through the Dublin traffic. Tess looked out of the window at the passing streets, but she wasn't really seeing them. She was hoping that the boy would not be waiting for her when she got off the bus. She didn't want to have to face him again.

He had been there for the first time on Wednesday, and then again yesterday. Both times he had done the same thing: he had started walking when she got down from the bus and had kept pace with her on the opposite side of the street until she turned into her own road at the edge of the park. She could feel his eyes on her almost constantly, but every time she glanced across he looked away. If she quickened her pace, he quickened his. If she stopped and pretended to examine something in the hedge, he stopped as well, always watching. It was almost as if he were teasing her and it unnerved her.

Tess sighed, pulled the elastic band from the end of her French braid, releasing her long dark hair from its confinement. It was Friday, and there were two whole days of freedom ahead. She wanted to enjoy the walk home in peace, so that she could make plans.

"Want a piece of gum?" said the girl sitting beside her. Tess smiled and shook her head. In a sense it was dishonest. She would have liked a piece of chewing gum. What she did not want was the embarrassment of someone trying to make friends with her. It was easier to stay out of it from the beginning, rather than face the disappointment that inevitably followed. Because she had been through it too often now to believe that things could ever be different. All her life her family had been on the move. A year here, two years there, following her father's promotions wherever they took him.

Tess had found it difficult at first but she had come to accept it as the years went by. Her parents encouraged her to make new friends wherever they were, and had even arranged parties for her, but they didn't understand. They couldn't. She went along with their parties and sometimes went as far as to invite someone home for a weekend to please them. But it was the best she could do. She had long ago come to realize that she would never really be able to make close friends. She was different and that difference was something that she would never be able to share with anyone.

The girl beside her got up as her stop approached. "Bye," she said. "See you Monday."

"See you," said Tess. There were still a few girls, like this one, who were making an effort to be friends, but it wouldn't last long. Soon she would be forgotten and ignored, dismissed as a grind or as too stuck-up to bother with. That was painful sometimes, but it was easier than having to pretend to be like everyone else.

The bus stopped and the girl got off, pulling on her gloves. Students from the local vocational school were around on the streets. They didn't have to wear uniforms, and they looked relaxed and human compared to the girls in her school with their matching overcoats and hats and shoes. Tess had wanted to go to the vocational school instead, but her parents had insisted that she should have the best available academic education. She had decided not to push it. They had taken her view into consideration when it came to the new house, and that was the most important thing.

The city traffic was always at its worst on Friday evenings, but at last the bus reached Tess's stop. She got off and walked a few yards along the main road. It was bitterly cold again and she was annoyed at herself for leaving her scarf at home. This freak weather had been going on for some time now, and there was no excuse for forgetting. She pulled up her collar and braced herself against the icy autumn breeze. As she turned into the tree-lined avenue which led to her road, she groaned inwardly.

He was there, leaning against the wall, waiting for her. There was no one else around. Tess walked quickly, looking firmly down at the ground. Today she would not be drawn in. She would not look over and give him the satisfaction of catching her eye. She watched the pavement stones intently and said to herself: "He doesn't exist. If I don't look at him, he isn't there."

But he was there, and today he was more there than ever. Out of the corner of her eye she saw him crossing over the street toward her, pushing his fair hair away from his eyes in a gesture that was already becoming familiar.

Her first instinct was to run, but she knew that it would be useless. She was strong, despite her small and wiry frame, and given the right circumstances she would be hard to beat over a short distance. But today she was wearing narrow shoes with heels, part of the ridiculous uniform, and her schoolbag was heavy. If he wanted to catch her she wouldn't have a chance, and if he was just trying to unnerve her, then he would succeed and she would look and feel like a fool. So she carried on walking but looked determinedly away from him, toward the houses.

He walked on the very edge of the sidewalk but even so, Tess moved in toward the walls and hedges they were passing, as far away from him as possible. The street seemed endless.

"Cigarette?" he said.

"No."

"Ah. Don't smoke?"

"No."

"Very wise."

Tess glanced at him. He was holding a very crumpled pack from which he extracted an even more crumpled cigarette. She noticed that he had no gloves and wondered how he could bear to have his hands out in the cold. In the brief instant that she looked at him, he caught her eye with a sly, sideways glance. His eyes were slate gray and very hard. They made her nervous.

Tess raised a hand to her hair, aware that it was still crinkly from the pressure of the braid. "What do you want?" she said.

"Oh, nothing much," he said. "What's your name?"

"None of your business."

He stopped abruptly to light his cigarette, and quite automatically, Tess stopped, too. She caught herself and went on again immediately, but it was too late. He would take it as a sign of acceptance and encouragement, and that was the last thing she wanted.

The Irish summer usually extended well into September, but this year the strange weather was bringing an early autumn to the country. Leaves swirled in the wind, many of them still green. Even with her fleece-lined gloves and thick tights, Tess was feeling the cold. The wind stung her cheeks, giving them a color that they usually lacked. Tess adjusted the shoulder-straps of her schoolbag and tucked her cold hands into her armpits.

The boy caught up with her in a few strides, light-footed in his worn sneakers. For a while he said nothing, puffing at his cigarette, concentrating on getting it going. Tess stole a glance at him out of the corner of her eye. He wore an army parka, frayed around the cuffs, and a pair of dirty jeans. He was older than she was, fourteen or fifteen perhaps, but he wasn't any taller. If he was going to give her any kind of trouble she thought she could probably hold him off until someone came out of one of the houses. Assuming they did. But what could he possibly want with her, anyway? Money? He certainly looked as if he were short of it.

"It might be, and it might not," he said.

"What?"

"Your name might be my business and it might not."

Tess glared at him and he looked nervously away.

He went on. "Mine is Kevin. Or Kev. Take your pick."

"No, thanks," said Tess.

He laughed, then, a high-pitched, musical laugh. Suddenly, Tess had had enough. She stopped in her tracks and turned on him, no longer uncomfortable, just furious.

"What do you want?" she shouted. "Why don't you just leave me alone?"

He jumped and stopped dead. Tess took advantage and walked quickly away, but he caught up with her. They were getting close to the edge of the park where Tess's house was.

"Don't be like that," he said. "I just want your help, that's all."

"Well, you can't have it," she said, more confident now that she was nearly home. "I don't have any help to offer."

The corner drew nearer. She would soon be home.

"Perhaps you do," said Kevin, walking closer now, and Tess thought she detected a hint of urgency in his voice. She noticed that he seemed to be constantly glancing around him, as though he were afraid of being seen. She wondered if he were on drugs, or if the police were after him.

"If you want help so badly," she said, "you should ask my father." As she spoke she heard herself using a tone she despised, the snooty little rich girl, the spoiled brat. But she couldn't stop herself. She turned toward him, her dark eyes taking on an expression of disdain, and said: "Or shall I ask him for you?"

They were at the corner. When he had followed her before, the boy had given up at this point and gone in the opposite direction. She felt confident he wouldn't follow her today. But as she started to turn the corner, he caught hold of her arm. She shook herself free, but he darted around and stood in front of her, his hair flopping into his eyes again.

"Wait," he said.

She stepped aside and went past him.

"What if I told your father about you?" he said.

A cold chill ran up Tess's spine. She stopped and turned back. Kevin was standing still. His face showed the tension he was feeling, but for the first time he was looking her straight in the eye.

"What do you mean?" she said.

"I know about you," he said. "I know what you do."

The chill spread, prickled through the base of her

brain and into her temples. She was caught by his intense gaze, and for a moment she was helpless and afraid.

"I won't tell," he said, "but you must help." Tess turned away.

"I haven't the faintest idea what you're talking about," she said.

o w ʇ   ɹ ǝ ʇ d ɐ ɥ ɔ

On Saturdays it was traditional for Tess to go shopping with her parents. It was supposed to be the high point of the week, to wander around whatever town they were living in, buy what they needed, and have a terrific lunch at the best restaurant they could find.

Tess's parents often spoke about money being short, but Tess didn't really know what it meant. She knew only that from time to time she was embarrassed by the fact that she was one of the better-off girls in her school. Her father was hardworking and well paid. If there was something that Tess wanted, she generally got it.

On the whole, however, she didn't want all that much. Her parents saw her as a quiet child, perhaps too quiet, who was given to reading in her room after school and taking long walks in the countryside on weekends. During the holidays they saw little of her. She would set out on her walks after breakfast, whatever the weather, and return when she felt like it, often quite late, though seldom after dark. She didn't talk much about these walks, but her parents were proud of her knowledge of nature and in particular of wildlife. The last house they had lived in was on the edge of a small town. It had faced out into the open countryside, and Tess had loved it there. The Dublin park was a poor substitute, but it was better than nothing.

For Christmas one year her parents had bought Tess a bicycle and often she went cycling instead of walking. They had offered her riding lessons, too, with a view to buying her a pony of her own, but she had declined. "Ponies are such fun," she had said. "I couldn't bear to sit up on top of one and boss it around." So they had dropped the idea and left Tess to her own devices. They saw no reason to do otherwise because she seemed, despite her lack of friends, to be quite content with her life.

When they had learned they were to be transferred to Dublin, Tess's parents knew that it was going to be hard on Tess, but even so, they were unprepared for the strength of her reaction. She burst into tears when they told her and locked herself away in her room. When she came out, she refused to speak to them at all for several days, and her mother came as close as she ever did to losing her temper.

Eventually, Tess capitulated and agreed to move to

Dublin on the condition that they get a house beside the Phoenix Park, a huge area of grassland and woods where herds of deer roamed freely and all manner of wildlife flourished. It was a popular part of town and it looked for a while as though they wouldn't be able to find anything. Then, just as they were about to give up on the idea, an old but comfortable house came onto the market and they wasted no time in buying it.

Tess was delighted, and also greatly relieved. She would have gone out of her mind if she had to live hemmed in by houses. Her "walks" were the only thing that made the difference between happiness and misery in her life.

On that particular Saturday, her father had some work to do and told her that they would not be going into town before noon. Tess hid her delight. Now she would have the morning to herself. An unexpected bonus.

"All right if I go for a walk, then?" she said.

"Are you sure?" her mother asked. "It's bitterly cold out."

"I'll wrap up," said Tess.

She put on jeans and her new down jacket, hat, scarf, and gloves and went outside. The wind wasn't strong, but it was colder, if anything, than the day before. Tiny particles of ice drifted in it, not quite snow yet, but a warning of it.

Tess looked up and down the road. During the summer holidays, there wasn't a parking space to be had for miles along the edge of the park, but today there were few cars. One or two stalwart owners were walking their dogs, and a few determined-looking families were playing soccer or Frisbee, but mostly the park was deserted. In particular, to Tess's relief, there was no sign of Kevin. If he wasn't around today, the chances were good that he hadn't been in the area on other Saturdays either. And if he hadn't, then he couldn't have followed her to the secret place she had found, and he couldn't have seen what she did there.

She began to relax a little as she walked across the bare fields of the park. She had always been careful, after all; very, very careful. It was vital that no one should see her and she had always made sure that they didn't. Kevin had just been bluffing. It was a clever bluff, too, because what teenager has not done some-thing in their life that they would prefer their father not to know about? But a bluff was all it was, she was sure about that. If he tried to talk with her again, she would invite him to come home with her and see what he had to say to her father. There was no way he would come.

She felt better, even lighthearted, as she came to the wild part of the park. Sometimes, when the park was full of people, it was a little awkward getting into her secret place without being seen, but today there was nobody within sight at all.

Tess's den was in an area where clusters of small trees stood. Beneath and between them, plenty of brambles and other scrubby growth provided cover. Tess looked around carefully. A woman had come into view, walking an Irish wolfhound that bounded with graceless pleasure across the open space of the park. Tess knew how it felt. She had tried a wolfhound once.

To be extra safe, Tess walked around her favorite copse and peered into one or two of the neighboring ones as well. The woman and the wolfhound were gone, but there was always a chance that somebody might be approaching, hidden by the trees. She stood still and listened for a long time. She knew the ways of the birds and small creatures well enough now to understand their voices and their movements. There was nothing to suggest that anyone apart from herself was making them uneasy.

She looked around one last time, then slipped into the copse that contained her hideaway. It was a place where she would not care to come alone at night.

Even in broad daylight it was dark in there, and a little eerie. There were light paths through it that were clearly used quite often, and scattered here and there throughout the undergrowth were fast-food wrappers and empty cans and bottles. Tess went on toward the middle, standing on brambles that crossed her path and ducking beneath low branches until she came to a place where the trees thinned a little. Here the undergrowth had grown up taller and thicker because of the extra light. A long time ago, a fairly large tree had fallen here, and the brambles had grown up around its remains. The smallest branches had rotted away, but the bigger ones were still intact and made a kind of frame.

Tess looked and listened one last time before she stooped and crawled into the narrow passage which she had made on previous visits. At the end of it was a small clearing in the undergrowth, sheltered from the wind and human eyes by a thick wall of brambles. When she came out, she was a squirrel, full of squirrel quickness and squirrel nervousness, darting and stopping, listening, darting again, jumping.

Everything and anything in life was bearable as long as she had this. What did it matter if she had to wear that absurd uniform and go to that snooty school? On the weekends she could be squirrel, or cat, or rabbit, or lolloping wolfhound, or busy, rat-hunting terrier. What did it matter if that disturbing boy was pestering her, trying to scare her? What did he know of the freedom of the swift or the swallow? What did he know of the neat precision of the city pigeon, or the tidiness of the robin or the wren? She would call his bluff and let him bully someone else. But just now, she would forget him as she forgot everything when she was a squirrel, because squirrel hours are long and busy and full of forgetfulness.

The sun poked through the branches above, and if it wasn't the warm autumn sun it might have been, it didn't matter so much. Its bright beams added to the dizzying elation of scurrying around and jumping from branch to branch, and Tess was too busy to be cold.

Squirrels do as squirrels must. It didn't matter that she would not be there to hibernate during the winter. Autumn was collecting time, so collect is what she did. But because she wouldn't have to eat her store of foodstuffs in the winter, it didn't particularly matter what she collected. Some things, like rose-hip seeds and hazelnuts, seemed urgent and could not be resisted. She stuffed the pouches of her cheeks and brought the food to her den. Other things, like sycamore wings and the mean, sour little blackberries that the cold, dry autumn had produced, were less urgent, but she brought them anyway because they looked nice and there wasn't anything else in particular to be done. If the other squirrels found her habits strange, they were too busy with their own gathering to give her their attention. The only time they bothered her was when she ventured too far into someone else's territory, and then a good scolding was enough to put her right.

She knew most of the other squirrels. Earlier in the year, before school started, she had often spent time playing with them, engaging in terrific races and tests of acrobatic skill. She always lost, through lack of coordination or lack of nerve, but it didn't matter. It was sheer exhilaration to move so fast, faster than her human mind could follow, and to make decisions in midair using reflex instead of thought. She remembered some of those breathtaking moments as she encountered particular squirrels, but there was no time for that kind of thing now. Life was rich with a different kind of urgency. Food was going to be scarce this winter.

There was a clatter of wings in the treetops. For an instant the thicket froze like a photograph, and then its movement began again. Nothing more than a gray pigeon making a rather clumsy landing. Tess caught a brief glimpse of something shining on the ground and swooped down a tree trunk headfirst to investigate. At first she thought it was a ring tab from a soda can, but as she got closer she saw that it was a real ring, a broad band of silver, scarcely tarnished at all. The metal grated unpleasantly against her little teeth, but she was determined to have it. She took a firm grip on it and pulled, but it would not come free. A sharp blade of tough grass had grown up through it and become entwined with other grasses on the other side. She tugged again, and all at once was aware of another of those sudden woodland silences that always spell a warning.

She froze. She could see no enemy, but she smelled him, and he was close, very close. It was a smell she had never encountered before. She looked around carefully and found herself face-to-face with the strangest squirrel she had ever seen. He was small and strong, his ears were sharp and pointed, and he was red with black and white stripes running down his back. Every other squirrel in the copse was still, looking down at this oddity

He's not a squirrel at all, thought Tess. He's a chipmunk. To her squirrel mind, this seemed perfectly reasonable, but her human mind was surprised: There are no chipmunks in Ireland!

Before she had time to think about it, the chip-

18

munk darted forward and took hold of the ring in his teeth. As though reassured by this, the other squirrels relaxed and went back about their business. But Tess was infuriated. Whatever he was, wherever he came from, this chipmunk was not going to have her ring.

She sprang forward and, standing next to him, she took a grip on the ring. It may have seemed like a courageous thing for her to do, to take on this intruder, but she was supported by the knowledge that if she were in real danger all she had to do was to change back into Tess. Not only would she escape, but she would give her enemy the fright of his life.

Once, when she had been a rabbit at dusk, not far from their last house, a fox had appeared from nowhere. She had fled with the other rabbits toward their burrows. But the rabbit in front of her had been slow to get in and the fox had been just about to close his teeth on her thigh. Instead, he was brought up short by a human leg, and he ran away home extremely frightened and bewildered.

She had been lucky. There had been no one around to see it happen. Changing back was a last resort, but here in the darkness of the thicket she was prepared to do it if she had to.

But she didn't. As soon as she took hold of the ring, the chipmunk released it and used its teeth instead to cut through the tough grass. The ring came free, and Tess raced off along the thicket floor, holding her head high so that the ring would not get snagged on plants or fallen twigs. The chipmunk followed. At the mouth of the passage that led to her den, Tess dropped the ring and scolded him soundly. He backed off some distance and sat on the stump of the fallen tree, watching her with a sly gleam in his eye that was disturbingly familiar. Tess picked up the ring and marched in through the tunnel entrance, then went into the deepest corner of the bramble patch and dropped it there behind a big stone. But when she turned around, she found the chipmunk right behind her, watching every move she made. She sprang at him, chattering and scolding as loudly as she could, and he bolted away toward the light at the tunnel entrance.

Tess turned back to find another hiding place for the ring, but no sooner had she done so than the chipmunk was there with her again, his tail high behind him, darting this way and that, always just out of reach of her teeth. For all the world he was behaving like a young puppy who wanted to play.

Tess stopped haranguing him and watched. Perhaps chipmunks weren't busy gathering at this time of year? Or perhaps he had escaped from a zoo or a private collector, and didn't know what he was supposed to be doing. Cautiously, she followed him.

When she reached the end of the tunnel, he bounded off and leaped halfway up the trunk of a tree and then down again. He raced back to her and then off again, into the branches this time, tempting her, teasing her.

And why not, she thought, why shouldn't she play? There was no need for her to be gathering. She followed, slowly at first, until she gained confidence and ran beside him. Now they were off, speeding along together through the trees and across the open spaces between them. They went from thicket to thicket, exploring them all at the highest possible speed, and from time to time they raced out onto the open part of the park, running and jumping through the tangled grasses as far as they dared, then returning helter-skelter to the safety of the trees.

Tess gave herself over completely to the game and the joy of companionship. It happened occasionally that she met a friend of a sort in the animal world, but as with human friends, it always seemed to be hard work. This was different. The chipmunk was as eager for company as she was. This time it was he who had found her and asked her to play. She couldn't remember when she had last felt so happy, and she didn't try. There was only now, the perfect moment, and it went on and on and on.

Until, suddenly, Tess caught sight of the sun. She had forgotten why, but she knew that it was much far-

21

ther across the sky than it ought to be. She stopped on a branch, her whiskers twitching, trying to quiet her flighty little squirrel brain so that she could think. All that came into her head were nuts, and a strong and compelling need to return to her den.

She raced pell-mell back to the copse and the fallen tree. The chipmunk followed, still trying to play.

As soon as she was in the den, she remembered. The trip to town. She didn't know the time but she knew that it was late, very late. Her parents would be anxious, perhaps angry, and it wouldn't be at all easy to come up with a believable excuse. The chipmunk had followed her into the den. With all the squirrel fury she could muster she turned on him and drove him out. He hovered at the door, looking perplexed, but she sprang at him again, chasing him farther away. Then she raced back into the darkness and, before he had time to follow her, she made the change. As she crawled out of the den on her hands and knees she expected to see him running away in terror, but there was no sign of him. None at all.

Halfway home across the park Tess realized that she had forgotten the ring. She sighed. It would be there tomorrow. If she wanted something to worry about, she need only think of her parents waiting for her.

22

c h a p t e r   t h r e e

When Tess arrived home, breathless and contrite, her mother said, "Never mind. If your father hadn't been working this morning, none of this would have happened."

Her father was silent. He had become involved in watching an international football game on TV, so Tess and her mother took a bus to the center of the city and had tea together. Afterward they split up to do a bit of shopping. Tess spent some of her allowance on a book about rodents that had a whole chapter on chipmunks, and the rest on a huge bag of sunflower seeds.

When they got back, Tess went upstairs and lay on her bed intending to read the rodent book. She was so exhausted by her squirrel adventures that she fell asleep and didn't wake up until her father called her down for dinner. During the week the family ate formally around the dining room table, but quite often on weekends they ate in front of the living room fire with trays on their knees. Tess sat down in an armchair and picked up her knife and fork. Her parents were watching a soap opera on TV, but it was one that she didn't follow. Her mind returned to the strange boy and to the secret that she had kept hidden for so long. She remembered the first time she had switched and discovered that she did not always and evermore have to be just Tess.

She had been quite small, just seven or eight, and she had woken unusually early on a summer's morning because she was uncomfortably hot. There were strange dream images in her mind; animal sounds and smells, sensations that she didn't recogize, but they receded before she could capture them. She sighed, and it seemed to her as she did so that time had slowed down. The sigh took forever, both coming and going, as though there were room in her lungs for more air than she had thought.

Outside, the birds were singing unusually loudly, and the sun was streaming through a gap in the curtains and onto her bed. She realized that this was probably why she felt so hot, but when she lifted her hand to throw back the covers, something brown and furry jumped up onto her chest.

Tess was not a screamer, even at that age, which was probably just as well. If she had attempted to scream at that moment, the noise might have awakened half the neighborhood. Instead she had stayed motionless for a long, long time, waiting for the creature to show itself again. When it did not, she began to relax a little. Slowly, carefully, Tess sat up. As she did so, she could see that the furry thing was still there on the top of her quilt.

In slowly dawning horror, Tess realized that it was not a small creature, but the paw of a very, very large one. She swung around, expecting to see the rest of the beast crouching on the floor beside her bed, but there was nothing there. And as she turned back, she knew. She lifted her hand, and there was no hand, just the great brown paw lifting to her face to feel the long snout and the round, furry ears. Tess had turned into a bear.

For a long time she stayed still. She had read about such things in fairy tales. Tears of hopelessness rolled down her hairy cheeks and spilled onto the quilt, making a dark patch that widened and widened. She listened to the birds, wondering how they could sound so joyful when she felt so sad. She might have stayed there indefinitely, weeping a great stain into the quilt, were it not that bears find it uncomfortable to lie on their backs for so long.

Her fingers would not work properly. The quilt snagged in her claws as she tried to push it off, but she managed to get herself disentangled and scrambled down onto the floor. It was surprising to find how comfortable a bear can be, and for a while she just ambled here and there around the room, getting accustomed to her strange limbs.

After a time the sound of the birds and the fresh scent of the morning drew her to the window. On the third attempt, her clumsy paw caught the curtain and pushed it to the side. Tess stood on her hind legs and leaned against the windowsill, blinking in the bright light. The smell, the sound, the feeling of the fresh air in her nostrils was so delicious, it was almost magical. She was filled with delight at being a bear and she stretched her nose up toward the cool gap where the window was open. Just at that instant, however, she caught a new scent, and then a glimpse, of the paper-boy cycling down the road.

As quickly as she could, Tess dropped back to the floor and away from the window. The horror of the situation returned. What on earth was going to happen to her?

From the room beside hers, she heard her parents' alarm clock ringing and she put her heavy paws up to her ears in dread. Any minute now she would hear her father padding along to the bathroom to wash and shave, and then he would open the door and say, "Rise and shine," or "Show a leg." Sometimes he came in and drew the curtains. Sometimes he even sat down on her bed and chatted for a while before he went down and put on the kettle. But what was going to happen now? What would he do when he saw, instead of his little girl, a brown bear?

He was humming now in the bathroom as he shaved. Would her mother be more likely to understand? If she looked her carefully in the eye, would she recognize her own Tess?

Tess shambled miserably around the room, feeling huge and heavy and clumsy. As she went by it, she knocked over the dolls' house. The noise that it made as it landed scared her, and she jumped and collided with a box of Legos. The pieces spilled out all over the floor and as Tess walked around, their sharp edges hurt her paws.

The bathroom door clicked shut. Tess heard her father's footsteps in the hall. She sat down in the middle of the room and prayed with all her might to be a little girl again.

The door opened. "What's all the noise about?" said her father.

Tess sat still and looked carefully up toward the door.

"What have you been doing?" her father said, as he came into the room.

Tess stared at him in astonishment. How could he not have noticed?

"Are you all right, sweetheart?" he said, squatting on his heels beside her.

She stared wide-eyed into his face, then looked down at her hands. She was Tess again, sitting on the floor in her nightdress, all warm and pink and human.

"I was a bear a minute ago," she said.

"A bear!" said her father. "Well. No wonder you made such a mess." He righted the dolls' house and began putting the things back into it.

"But I was, Daddy, I really was."

"Well, you'd better be a tidy little squirrel now and pick up all those Lego bricks before your mom sees them. You can pretend they're all nuts."

"But I wasn't pretending," said Tess.

"Of course you weren't."

"Do you believe me?"

"Of course I do."

But she knew by the tone of his voice that he didn't. Changing into bears just wasn't the kind of thing that adults did. They would be far too worried about what other people were thinking. So when, a few weeks later, Tess turned herself into a cat, she promised herself that she would never, never tell anyone ever again. And she never did.

That boy, that scruffy Kevin character, he couldn't know. He just couldn't. It wasn't possible. All the same, there was something about the way he had looked at her that scared her and made her almost believe that he did, somehow, know what she could do.

"Tess."

"Yes?"

"You're not eating your dinner, sweetheart."

"Oh. I was just listening to the news." She hadn't been, but she started to now.

"Meanwhile," said the TV newscaster, his face impressively grave, "the freak weather conditions continue. The snowstorms that have been ravaging the Arctic regions for the past eight weeks show no signs of abating, and their area of activity continues to increase. The death toll in northern Europe now stands at more than seventeen hundred, and there are many more people unaccounted for. Evacuations continue across the Northern Hemisphere."

The TV screen showed a picture of a line of cars driving through a blizzard.

"Inhabitants of Alaska and northern Canada continue their southward exodus as weather conditions make their homes uninhabitable. Air rescue teams are working around the clock to move people from outlying areas, and snowplows are working twenty-four hours a day to keep the major routes clear."

"There's something fishy about all this," said Tess's father.

"Fishy?" said her mother. "How can there be something fishy about the weather?"

"I don't know, but it isn't natural."

"How can the weather not be natural?" her mother asked. "If the weather isn't natural, what is?"

"Well, it's not normal, anyway."

"Normal is a different question entirely. No one is saying this is normal."

"Shhh!" said Tess.

"The fourth land attempt to reach the weather-bound Arctic oil-drilling station has had to be abandoned," said the newscaster above pictures of army snowmobiles and tanks. "Radio contact with the drilling rig was lost soon after the storm conditions began, and successive attempts to reach it by air and by land have failed."

An army officer appeared on the screen, dressed like a Himalayan mountaineer. Snowflakes whirled around him.

"It's just impossible out there," he said. "Conditions like these have never been encountered before. The temperatures are falling off the bottom of the thermometer and visibility is nil. With the best will in the world it is not feasible to expose army personnel to such conditions."

Tess thought he looked scared.

"I still say it's fishy," said her father.

Her mother sighed in exasperation. Tess stood up with her tray. "I'm going upstairs to read," she said.

"Don't you want any dessert?" said her mother. "It's lemon meringue."

"I'm not hungry," said Tess. "Perhaps you could leave me a piece for later?"

Tess took her tray out to the kitchen and went back to her room. No one was saying it, but it was on everybody's mind. If those snowstorms continued to spread, it would not be long before they reached Ireland. And then what would it matter if that stupid boy did or didn't know her secret?

# c h a p t e r   f o u r

c h a p t e r   f o u r

In a conference room in the United Nations building in New York City, the same army officer who had made an appearance on Tess's TV was sitting at an oval table beside his commanding officer, General "Watchdog" Barker. Nine other seats at the table were occupied by members of the recently formed Intergovernmental Panel on Climate Change. There were no members of the public or the press among them.

The officer, whose name was Captain Miller, passed his cap from hand to hand in a gesture of restlessness. At his right hand was a large, square tape recorder, and in front of him, covering most of the tabletop, was a huge map of the Arctic Circle. As his CO rose to his feet, Miller straightened up in his seat. The general cleared his throat. "Ladies and gentlemen," he said. "We are here to submit evidence to the panel. With your leave, we won't waste time." There was a general murmur of assent among the assembled deputies. Captain Miller rose to his feet and slipped a small tape into the machine.

"This message," he said, "is the last one that our Arctic Surveillance Station in northern Alaska received from the workers on the polar drilling rig, a week after they were marooned by the storms. I think it's worth saying that we have no reason to believe that this transmission was received by anybody else apart from ourselves." He switched on the machine. The reception was poor and full of crackling static but nonetheless voices could be heard.

"Yeah, boys, we're still okay here." It was the voice of a young man, a bit of a wise guy, but putting a brave face on a difficult situation.

"Nothing to report?" said the radio officer from the Arctic Surveillance Station.

"Yeah, a lot to report. But it's all snow, you know? A hell of a lot of it."

"How's the platform holding up?"

"I guess it's okay. The winds are as high as ever, you know? There's a lot of creaking and groaning going on, it's pretty scary sometimes, but I don't think there's been any more damage since last Tuesday."

"Do you have enough supplies?"

"Yep. We're having a ball, you know?"

"So morale is okay?"

"Good enough. We . . ." Here there was a loud bang. "Whoops! Someone in a hurry with the coffee."

Now there were excited voices in the background, but only the louder exclamations were picked up clearly by the radio mike. "But it's massive, man" and "I swear to God it's moving." Then the young man came back to the mike. "Hey, I gotta go for a minute. The guys are kind of worked up. Cabin fever, I guess. I got to go and take a look. Will you hold on to the line there for a minute?"

"Sure, but what's happening?"

"I'll get right back to you. Don't go away, now."

There was a long pause, during which nothing could be heard except the hiss and crackle of static. At the United Nations, the listeners around the table shifted in their seats. Then there was a second bang, like the first, followed a moment later by a series of loud metallic groaning and grating sounds, and then there was nothing. The radio connection went dead.

Captain Miller took the tape out of the machine and slipped it back into his pocket. "We don't know any more than you do," he said to the assembled deputies. "We have not had any more radio contact with the polar drilling rig. Air rescue is impossible in those conditions, as General Barker will confirm." Captain Miller looked toward Barker, who nodded.

"There are gale-force winds out there that change direction every couple of minutes," said General

Barker. "Nothing can fly accurately. And as you know, we sent in land teams, but those have failed as well."

He nodded to Miller, who produced a second tape.

"This tape is the last record we have of the snowmobile mission."

Miller put the second tape into the machine. This time the line was a lot clearer. "Still moving along," said a young man's voice. "Ground's pretty level. Harry's taking a nap."

"No, sir," said Harry. "Just resting my eyes as per orders."

"Yeah," said the first speaker. "It's hard on the eyes all right. I've got little white worms running across mine. How come I can see white worms when everything else is white?"

"Have they got black edges?"

"Let me see. Yeah. I think they have black edges." He laughed. "But they won't keep still and let me look at them." There was a pause, then the same voice continued. "Any news at your end?"

"No. Everything's pure white and deadly boring."

"Oh, well. At least we're not missing . . . Hey! Whoa! What the hell is that?"

"What's up?" said Harry. "Hey! Stop, Bill."

Bill's voice was suddenly full of terror. "We have

stopped, blast it. It's that thing that's moving! Oh, my God. It's alive!"

There was a single scream that sent a chill of horror through the listeners at the United Nations, and then the tape went as dead as the first one. The silence spread to the listeners. After a long time, Captain Miller cleared his throat.

"We didn't regain contact with that snowmobile or the other one. I called off the mission immediately and brought the team back home as quickly as I could. With the weather as bad as it is now, we can't maintain the base in Barrow any longer, and we've pulled all our men out of the area. I think I should say here that we have no plans to make any further excursions into the region as long as current weather conditions continue."

The deputy from Sweden broke into the silence that followed.

"If I can just try to clarify things here," she said. "Are we to understand that there's something living out there in the middle of those storms?"

"We're not in a position to say that," said General Barker. "We have no more evidence than what you have just heard."

There was a long, heavy silence. It was broken, at last, by the French representative.

"Might I suggest," he said, "that we have a matter here that demands the attention of the Security Council?"

There was another silence. Then, one after another, the delegates gave their assent.

The next morning, Tess slept late and had a leisurely breakfast. The mood in the house was low, and Tess knew that it was not just because yesterday did not go as planned. Even her father could not raise his customary cheerful Sunday spirit.

It was this weather. There was no change, and the radio reports gave no indication that there was likely to be one. The meteorologists admitted that they were baffled. Satellite pictures revealed nothing. The Arctic storms were gradually spreading southward. There had been no rain since the day it started to get so cold, and now the radio gave the first warnings of possible water shortages. It wasn't yet necessary to introduce rationing, but people were being asked to reduce their consumption as much as possible.

The whole business made Tess gloomy. She was still a bit tired, too, from her wild antics as a squirrel during the previous day. But she wrapped herself up well and set out across the park with the sunflower seeds under her arm.

The scene was similar to the day before. Only the few who refused to be defeated by the weather had made it to the park. Tess wound her scarf around her face and breathed through the wool. From time to time she jogged to keep warm.

When she got to her favorite part of the park, she opened her bag and wandered through the thickets, scattering sunflower seeds as she went. She listened to the sounds of the birds and small animals, and laughed a little at their mixture of suspicion and delight. When the bag was empty, she checked the surroundings carefully and went quietly into her den.

Tess was completely adept at changing now. It had taken a lot of practice, and when she was younger there had been times when she couldn't make it work. Switching required a state of mind that was somehow more, and somehow less, than just thinking. First, she needed to know what she wanted to be and had to have a clear picture in her mind of whatever creature it was. Next, and more difficult, she had to try to imagine how it felt to be that creature from the inside. Then she had to let go.

Letting go was the most difficult part, because the instant of changing was a bit scary. For that moment, brief though it was, it felt as though her mind were dissolving, and everything around her became vague and fluid and insubstantial. Once that moment had passed, everything was fine again. She took on the being of whatever she had become, and that existence was as real to her as her usual human one. But there had been times, in the past, when she had failed to change because she had shied away at the last moment from that frightening instant of dissolution and clung to what was certain and safe.

Over the years, Tess had discovered that thought, concentration, and anxiety were all hindrances to the process of change. Now she dispensed with them and simply plunged, spontaneously, into any shape she fancied. In the dark of previous dens, Tess had experienced the nature of most of the wild and domesticated creatures in Ireland, and most of the more common birds as well. She knew now, beyond all doubt, that she could be anything she wanted to be.

As soon as she was a squirrel again, Tess set out in search of the chipmunk. There was no sign of him in the immediate vicinity, so she scampered into the trees and hunted through the branches. But it soon became hard to keep her mind on what she was doing. All the other squirrels were frantic with activity, gathering the sunflower seeds she had scattered and bringing them home to their nests. For a while she resisted the temptation to join them but in the end it proved too strong for her. She knew that she had brought those seeds and she knew that she had no need to make a winter store, but the instinct of a beast is strong, and soon Tess gave in and joined them.

It filled her squirrel heart with joy to find food so plentiful. She filled her little cheeks until they bulged, and scurried back to her den time after time. All around her the other squirrels and the birds and the field mice were delighted by the unexpected windfall, and Tess knew that her allowance had never been better spent.

Still there was no sign of the chipmunk. Every now and then Tess remembered him and leaped up into the treetops to see if she could see him from there. Then she would go back to work and forget him again.

The day drew on and Tess had a fine heap of sunflower seeds in her den. She realized that it would soon be time to go home, and it was then that she thought, for the first time, of the silver ring. Hurriedly, she unloaded her cheeks and skipped across to the dark corner where she had left it. The stone was there, big and solid, and she searched around behind it but there was no sign of the ring. Tess sat down and thought as hard as a squirrel can think, but both her squirrel mind and her human mind were sure that she had left the ring just there, behind the stone. She searched again, and when she still didn't find it, she searched all the corners of the den, pushing aside the rotten leaves and twigs with her nimble squirrel fingers and feeling around where it was too dark to see. All at once Tess knew that the chipmunk had taken the ring. She stopped still and tried hard not to believe it but she knew that it was true. He had been such a friend, such a good friend, but now he had let her down by taking her ring and disappearing. It filled her heart with such sadness that she didn't want to become Tess again, because she knew that most of the creatures of the earth feel sadness from time to time, but only humans collect it like a store of nuts and feel the need to make it last.

But she had to be herself again. There was homework to be done for tomorrow, and then another week of school before she could be here again, and free. She changed before she had time to think about it. With a human hand she reached behind the stone and felt around carefully, but there was no doubt now that the ring was gone. The little heap of sunflower seeds that had seemed so huge and satisfying to her squirrel self looked small now and pathetic. She brushed them into the palm of her hand and scattered them on the floor of the thicket as she set off for home.

# chapter five

chapter five

**M**onday dragged on, as it always did. Tess had brought her rodent book to school, and read it secretly during math and religion, but since the disappearance of the ring it had lost its appeal. There were no references to wild chipmunks in Ireland, or any suggestion that chipmunks were interested in collecting baubles.

The other girls in Tess's class had come to accept that she preferred to keep to herself. She knew that it would be hard to make up all that lost ground if she ever changed her mind and wanted to make friends, but she had created an image for herself in the school and for the moment she was content to leave things as they were. But that evening, when a photocopied letter was handed to each girl to take home to her parents, she rather wished that she was free to join in the celebrations that followed. The letter read:

> Dear Parent,
> Owing to the prevailing weather condi-

*tions, the girls will not be required to wear their school uniforms until further notice.*

*Yours sincerely,*

*M. L. Harvey, Principal*

Tess almost got off the bus at a stop before her own. She knew that there had to be a way through to the park from there, and once she had reached it, she couldn't go wrong. She pictured that stupid Kevin's face as he realized she wasn't on the bus. He could stand there and freeze for all she cared. But at the last minute, Tess's courage failed her and she stayed on the bus. She might be the one who got frozen if she lost her way and had to wander around the streets for too long.

When she got off at her own stop, Tess's heart sank. He was on her side of the street this time, leaning against the wall with his hands in his pockets, watching for her. She noticed that his face brightened for an instant the moment he caught sight of her, but then it took on that familiar, shifty expression. Tess thought of crossing the street, but she knew it was useless. Instead she looked straight ahead and walked briskly past. Kevin fell into step beside her. After a minute of silence, he said, "Ready to tell me your name yet?"

Tess swung around and faced him. "Look, why don't you just clear off and leave me alone!" She was shouting louder than she meant to, and a woman on the other side of the street gaped at them as she passed.

Kevin looked away, to hide the apprehension in his face. After a minute or two, he said, "What kind of manners are those?"

"What would you know about manners?" said Tess. "With your whining and scrounging."

"Scrounging?" said Kevin. "Who's scrounging?"

"What are you doing then, if you're not scrounging?" asked Tess.

Kevin sighed deeply and took out a cigarette. "You're being ridiculous, you know," he said.

"Listen to who's talking! I've already told you I don't want anything to do with you. You're not getting my name and you're not getting any money, either. If you want to get something, then get lost."

Kevin laughed. "That's a good one," he said. "Did you think of that one on the spot?"

Tess didn't know whether to be infuriated or flattered, and when Kevin stopped and turned to the wall to light his cigarette, she almost stopped as well. But she didn't get caught this time. Instead she quickened her pace, almost to a run. Kevin caught up. "You won't help, then?" he said.

"No."

"But you don't even know what I'm asking you for."

"Whatever it is I haven't got it. And if I had I wouldn't give it to you."

"But you have got it. In fact, you're the only one who has."

"Rubbish."

They were walking so fast now that they were nearly at the edge of the park. Suddenly, Kevin dodged in front of Tess and blocked her way. She tried to sidestep but he threw away his cigarette and grabbed hold of her shoulders. She was shocked at the sudden movement and surprised by his strength, but it was the look on his face that stopped her from trying to break away. There was no slyness there now, no fear. He was looking at her straight on, and his eyes were bright and keen and completely serious.

"Is it really possible," he said, "that you haven't worked this out yet?"

Tess tried to think of something clever to say, but she couldn't. For some reason she knew it wasn't the time for being clever. Kevin spoke slowly, as though she were a rather dim child. "Do you really believe that there are chipmunks in the Phoenix Park?"

Tess felt her mouth drop open. Her mind flew back to Saturday. She had been so careful. It was impossible that he had seen. He took his hands from her shoulders and blew on them to try and warm them. Tess remained motionless, openmouthed, staring. Kevin put his hands in his pockets, and the sly gleam returned to his eyes. And just as she remembered that same look in the bright little eyes of the chipmunk, Kevin took hold of her gloved hand and dropped something into it.

It was the silver ring.

Tess was afraid that her emotions would show on her face. All those years of silence and secrecy and guilt were over, and she was no longer alone. She almost hugged Kevin then, despite his scruffy clothes, but he began to talk before she had the chance.

"You'll help, then?" he said.

Tess was bewildered. "Help with what?"

"I'm not sure yet," said Kevin, gazing out across the park. "But if you meet me tonight we'll find out."

"Meet you? Where?"

"Connolly Station. One o'clock."

"One o'clock in the morning?"

"Is that too early?"

"Too early?"

"Use your head," he said. "You'll need time to get out, won't you? And you'll have to get there."

"But I can't," said Tess. "How can I?"

Kevin blew on his hands again and shrugged. "If you can't, you can't," he said, and he began to walk away. "But I'll be there anyway."

She watched him as he went. She knew nothing about him, nothing at all. Then she remembered the little chipmunk racing with her, playing, staying close, and she felt that she did know him, at least as well as she needed to.

"Kevin?" she called.

He turned back. "Yes?"

"My name is Tess."

He smiled and gave her a thumbs-up. But her heart was heavy as she walked towards her house. How could she possibly do as he asked?

# chapter six

c h a p t e r s i x

Tess lay awake, listening to her parents getting ready for bed. She could hear their voices through the wall, but not the words. The mumble was comforting, a background sound familiar as her own breathing, but it didn't make Tess any happier.

Kevin had asked her for help and she had let him down. The clock on the wall said twelve twenty-five. Even if she had the courage to cross the city at this hour, there was no way she could do it. The last buses would be on their way out of the center of town and they would not be returning until morning. A taxi, even if she could find one, would be too expensive. If she had meant to be there, she would have left an hour ago or more. But it was impossible. Couldn't he understand that? What parents would allow their thirteen-year-old daughter out in the dead of night to meet a boy they had never set eyes on?

If she had any friends she might, just might, have pretended to be staying with them. If for example she had gone with someone to a disco or a film, she could have gone on from there. But there was no one for her to go out with and nowhere to go.

She couldn't even sneak out. Just ten minutes ago her father had put his head around the door and listened, as he did every night. She had made her breathing as deep and regular as she could. It was dreadful, being an only child.

Twelve thirty-five. Poor Kevin. He would soon be arriving at Connolly Station, all alone among the homeless people and the winos, looking round for her, waiting. And here she was, lying in her comfortable bed, feeling wretched, feeble, worthless.

She turned over onto her side, but she knew she wouldn't be able to sleep for a long time. The clock on the wall ticked with infuriating monotony. Outside, an occasional car passed along the road, and in the tree opposite, a barn owl began to call.

Tess listened, pleased to hear the familiar sound. It seemed strange tonight, different somehow. Her nerves were on edge. She sighed and turned again in the bed.

"*What a fool,*" said the owl. "*What a foo-ool.*"

Tess sprang up, almost before she understood why. Of course! She would have laughed and shouted out loud if she hadn't been afraid of waking her parents. As quietly as she could, she opened the window and climbed up onto the sill. The freezing night air blew into the room. She wouldn't be able to close the window behind her, but it was too bad.

A moment later, a barn owl was speeding toward the center of the city, high above the houses and offices. It was a young owl, healthy and strong, and singularly delighted by the power of flight.

Tess knew Connolly Station well. Although they had lived in Dublin for less than three months, they had often visited the city in the past to do some special shopping or to go to a show or a play, and as often as not they had come by train.

It was easy enough for her to find the station from above. The city was spread out like a map beneath her, and once she had found the railway lines where they crossed the North Strand, she could not go wrong. The difficulty would be finding somewhere to land and change her shape without being seen. But her attention was drawn from the problem as she flew down over the station because she was joined by another owl. It swept in from somewhere above and behind her, and as it drew level it bumped into her and knocked her off balance, so that she fluttered wildly in the air for a moment or two. As soon as she was steady again, the other owl returned to fly beside her. Tess was afraid that she had broken some territorial rule and offended the other bird. It would not be a problem if it allowed her to fly away, but she was afraid that if it continued to be aggressive she would either fall or be forced too far away from the station to get to Kevin on time.

But it didn't collide with her again. Instead it flew alongside for a while, then moved a little ahead and veered across her so that she had to swing to her right. As soon as she did so, it dropped back beside her and turned its head carefully to look at her. It was then that Tess realized it was Kevin, and if an owl could have smiled, she would have. Instead, she nodded her head in recognition and he blinked three times, then flew on ahead. She followed as he swept over the bus station and the Custom House, then swung away from the river and back toward the North Side. They followed streets, which became darker and narrower, until they came to a few blocks of dilapidated flats built around dark, rectangular courtyards. Above the first of these they flew in diminishing circles until they were sure that no one was around, then Kevin dropped into the courtyard and swooped straight in through an open window on the second floor. It was a lovely piece of flying. Feeling slightly reckless, Tess let go and followed.

By the time she had got her bearings in the room,

Kevin had already turned back into human shape. Tess followed suit. As an owl, with her good night eyes, she had seen him quite clearly, but for a girl, the dark in the room was almost impenetrable. For a moment or two she was quite unnerved. The place smelled bad, of moldy mattresses and soot and stale beer. But there was something even worse.

"Kevin?" she said.

"Yes?"

"Can you see me?"

"Not really, no."

"I'm in my pajamas."

She heard his laugh ring out around the room. It was hard and scornful, and it hurt.

"Shut up," she said. "I didn't have to come here, you know. You don't know what it cost me to get here."

"What did it cost you?"

But she didn't tell him, because then he would know that it mattered to her not to let him down. Instead she said, as unkindly as she could, "Is this where you live, then? Is this your house?"

He struck a match and lit a candle and a cigarette from it. "I don't live anywhere," he said.

"Don't be stupid," said Tess. "Everyone lives some-where."

"Who's everyone?" he said.

Tess shivered. In the candlelight she could see the stained mattress in one corner, surrounded by a jumble of newspapers and empty cans and bottles. There was an untidy heap of dark blankets in another corner, but Tess would not have touched them, let alone put one around her shoulders.

"Do you live here?" she asked. "Seriously?"

"Of course not." Kevin sounded bitter. "What do you think I am?"

"Where do you live, then?"

"I already told you that."

"Then who does live here?"

"No one. Some old tramps use it sometimes, when they can't get into the hostel."

The cold was beginning to hurt. Kevin didn't seem to be aware of how bad it was. By the flickering light of the candle, she could see him looking from one corner of the room to another with that familiar nervousness. She was suddenly close to tears.

"What are we doing here?" she asked. "I don't understand any of this. How am I supposed to help you?"

Kevin shrugged. "I'm not even sure myself yet," he said, "but I know it's important. There's a rumor going around. The rats want to take me somewhere."

"Rats!"

"Yes. You got something against rats?"

Tess had. A rat was one of the things that she had never been and had no desire to be. But before she could say anything, Kevin went on:

"A rat is about the best thing to be in a city like this. They have the run of the place, you know? They never go hungry." He smiled at the distaste clearly evident on her face. "They have a lot of fun, too. More often than not I'm a rat."

He watched closely for her reaction. Tess tried not to show it. The idea filled her with unease. For although she had spent a lot of her time being all kinds of other creatures, she had never considered herself to be anything other than human. But if Kevin spent most of his time being a rat, then what did that make him? This theory explained the nervous way he behaved when he was human, as though there were always an enemy somewhere close at hand.

"Never been a rat, huh?" he said.

"No."

"Don't worry. You'll enjoy it. But there's quite a stir going on about this cold weather. At least, I think that's what it's about. Everybody's suffering, you know, not just the people. That's why I came looking for you. The rats want me to meet somebody. I don't know who this person is. All I know is that they live a long way from here."

As Tess watched him, the tense expression left his face and there was a momentary confusion in his eyes as he said, "I didn't want to go there on my own."

There were suddenly too many questions in Tess's mind. There was too much to share with this strange boy, and possibly too much to cope with. And it was too cold to face any of it.

"I have to go home," said Tess. "I have to get warm and think it over."

"But there's no time to think it over. This thing is important, Tess. This weather's getting worse all the time."

"Do you think I don't know that? Don't you realize I'm getting frostbite standing here?"

Kevin bit his lip. "I'm sorry," he said. "I wasn't thinking." He began to take off his coat.

"Don't be ridiculous," said Tess. "What difference does it make if you freeze instead of me? The point is, the whole thing sounds ridiculous to me. How can we possibly have any effect on the weather, whatever we do?"

"I don't know," said Kevin, zipping up his parka again, "but I do know this. Most of my life I've been going in and out of the animal world, and never before did they take any particular notice of me. But now they have. They know that I'm different and they're asking me for something."

"I'm too cold to think straight," said Tess. "I have to go home."

"But we can go right away," he said. "Come on. You won't be cold once we get moving." As he spoke, he was pointing toward a large hole beside the fireplace.

"As a rat?" said Tess.

"Of course."

Tess shook her head and at the same moment changed back into an owl. She hopped out of the window and flew straight up and away toward the park. Gradually the activity warmed her and she began to feel better. The whole idea was crazy. All she wanted to do was to curl up in her own bed and forget all about it. But she was not allowed to. As she landed lightly on the edge of her bedroom window, she realized that Kevin was right behind her.

c h a p t e r   s e v e n

Kevin and Tess stood in her room, facing each other.

"Good night, Kevin," said Tess.

"Oh. You're going to bed, are you?"

"Yes." She wanted to close the window on the night and all that was in it and allow the room to warm up, but she couldn't do that until he was gone. Instead, she climbed into bed and wrapped the covers around her.

Kevin wandered around the room, examining her things. It made Tess uncomfortable. It always made her uncomfortable when someone less well-off than she was came to the house. She had no pride in her standard of living, and in situations like this she felt rather guilty.

"You've got a lot of books," said Kevin.

"Observant, aren't you?" said Tess.

"Have you read them all?"

"Most of them."

He took a thick volume out of the bookcase and opened it. "You like mythology, then?"

"My dad does. He buys most of that stuff."

"Do you read it?"

"If I'm bored enough."

Kevin leafed through the book. "This is a good one," he said. "I haven't seen this one before."

Tess sighed and tried to drop him a hint by turning her face to the wall, but he went on, "I spend hours in the library, you know."

"Oh? When you're not rummaging through people's trash?"

She couldn't see him, but she could imagine the look on his face in the brief silence before he said, "Yes. Or raiding their kitchens or waking up their babies at night. Rats are okay, you know, you shouldn't underestimate them. They have their own codes of behavior, even if they're not like yours. They have a language, too."

"All animals do."

"No, not really. All animals have ways of communicating, but the rats actually have a language, a sort of visual language."

Tess said nothing, and Kevin continued to leaf through the book.

"I love all this stuff, though," he said at last. "All these heroes and gods and wonderful beasts. It's the best thing about people, if you ask me. Their imagination."

"I didn't ask you," said Tess, and as soon as she said

it, she regretted it. It was one step too far.

Kevin hurled the book across the room. It hit the wall above her head with a loud crack and landed on the pillow in front of her nose. She sat up.

"For God's sake, Kevin," she said, as loud as she dared. "You'll wake my parents!"

"Your parents? Your precious mummy and daddy? Who cares? Eh? As long as you're all right, all warm and cozy with your feather duvet and your central heating and your own private little life. The rest of the world can go hang, can't it, as long as you're all right!"

"Shh, Kevin, don't shout! I don't know what you want, can't you understand that? I don't understand what you're asking me to do."

"Nor do I!" said Kevin. "But I think that it's important. And even if it isn't, I have to find out." He came over to her and sat on the edge of the bed. Tess's nerves were on edge, waiting for the sound of her father's feet in the hallway.

"You have to help me, Tess," Kevin went on. "You just have to. I can't do this on my own. For one thing, I don't have very much time left."

"What do you mean?"

"It doesn't go on forever, you know, this thing, this ability we have. Did you know that?"

"No."

"Only until we're fifteen."

"How do you know?"

"Someone told me. She was one of us, too, but now she isn't. She learned it from another switcher. After her fifteenth birthday she couldn't change any-more. That's the end of it."

The news came as a blow to Tess. She had always believed that her gift would be with her for the rest of her life, the one thing she could be sure of.

"We all meet someone who tells us," said Kevin, "and we all meet someone we have to tell. I don't know how it works or why, but it seems that it always does. Anyway, the point is, I'm nearly fifteen, you know? And I'm nervous about what's happening."

"So you want me to come along and hold your hand?"

Kevin looked crestfallen, and suddenly Tess didn't know why she was putting up such a resistance and being so unkind. She lay back on the pillow to think about it and Kevin sat quietly, glancing at her from time to time in his nervous, sideways manner. Tess realized as she lay there that there was nothing to think about. If she refused to go with Kevin, she would never know what it was about and whether her gift had given her a part to play in some scheme or other. She would have to live with that uncertainty for the rest of her life. No matter how crazy it seemed, she had to go. There was no choice.

She sighed and threw back the covers. A look of delighted surprise crossed Kevin's face. He turned away quickly so that she wouldn't see it, but he couldn't disguise the spring in his step as he crossed the room. On top of her pajamas, she pulled on her jeans and then two sweatshirts, a thick sweater, and two pairs of socks. Kevin waited in her room as she crept downstairs, like a burglar in her own house, to get her down jacket and gloves.

Back in the bedroom, Tess hesitated. Whatever anxiety she had about the risk she might be running for herself was nothing compared to the feeling that gripped her now. She knew beyond any doubt that she would not be returning before morning, and that her parents would have to face the shock of coming in and finding her room empty. She felt sick, but there was no turning back. With hands that trembled more from tension than from cold, she searched through the drawers of her desk for some notepaper that her aunt had given her for Christmas. Then she sat down and picked up her pen.

The paper had delicate impressions of swans in blue and gold. Kevin leaned over her shoulder as she wrote. "Nice paper," he said.

"Shh."

"Dear Mummy and Daddy," she wrote. "I have to go away for a little while. I'm sorry, but I can't explain why. But you must trust me, just this once. Don't send anyone to search for me. It would only be a waste of time. I promise that I will take care of myself, and you must promise me that you will do the same and not worry too much. I will be back as soon as I can. Love you with all my heart, Tess, XXXXXXXX"

"Yuck," said Kevin. "All my heart."

Tess swung on him. "Shut up," she said in a vicious whisper. "Shut your filthy mouth. Just because you haven't got anybody."

He shrugged and turned away, and Tess was sorry, because she realized for the first time that it was true. He had nobody. Nobody at all.

She pinned the note to her pillow and took a last look around the room. Then side by side with Kevin, she walked to the window.

The two owls swept away again over the city. Kevin led the way back toward Connolly Station, but instead of returning to the flats, he headed for a small patch of wasteland in the same area. A row of houses had been demolished there to make way for some new building project which had never materialized. They flew over the area once or twice, checking it out, and then they began to descend.

There was a crowd of young men gathered around a car a couple of blocks away, but they were not close enough to be a danger. The owls flew a little lower over the waste ground again and, to Tess's horror, her sharp night eyes saw that the whole area was swarming with rats. There was a high chain-link fence around the plot, but nonetheless the local people had managed to turn the place into a dumping ground for their garbage. Mainly it was large things, old couches with the stuffing hanging out, broken TVs and refrigerators, and mattresses with bulging springs. But there were black plastic bags there as well, spilling out their contents of empty cans and vegetable peelings and tea bags. A perfect breeding ground for rats.

As the owls spiraled cautiously downward, there was a sudden flurry of rapid movement as the rats leaped for cover, followed by absolute stillness. Into this the two birds landed, and before Tess could even take a breath Kevin dissolved before her eyes and became a rat.

It was strange to watch it happening. If Tess had been asked, she probably would not have been able to describe what it looked like, because it looked, in a sense, just the way it felt. She had the same dizzying sensation of the world losing focus and becoming fluid, as though the observer also were drawn into the process of change and somehow became part of it. She watched as Kevin trotted away a little distance, then stopped and looked back. Tess stood still with her wings folded, looking around with large eyes that missed nothing, even in the darkness. The rats were everywhere, poking their noses out of the tin cans and paper bags and carpet folds where they had taken cover. Kevin sat up on his tail and twitched his whiskers with that same nervousness that carried into his human form. Tess wanted to be with him, but she was stuck. She just couldn't bring herself to make that change.

It wasn't only as a human that she hated rats. Every creature that she had ever been hated them, too. The birds hated them because they would raid any nest they could reach and whisk away a hatchling or fledgling that got out from under its parent's eye. Cats and dogs hated them because they were thieving and provocative, and because if they were hungry enough they would take even a young pup or kitten from its bed. Other scavengers hated them because they were greedy and aggressive and invariably got the better of an argument. Even the large and tolerant beasts like horses and cattle found rats distasteful because they respected neither peace nor privacy, and they fouled whatever fodder they were unable to eat.

Kevin came back toward her. The other rats, sensing that she was not a threat, had begun to emerge from their hideouts. She turned her head slowly from side to side. She was not afraid. An owl is a match for any rat. She watched them carefully, allowing her owl instinct to savor the idea of snatching the plumpest of them and flying with it to the nearest tree. But it was not to be. From the street came the soft *click-click* of a dog's claws on pavement stones. The rats froze. As Tess watched, the dog appeared at the chain-link fence and stopped, looking straight at her. For a long moment, nothing moved. Then the dog, with a single, soft bark, announced its intention and ducked through a gap in the fence.

Looking back, Tess could never understand exactly why she made the decision she did at that moment. It would have been as easy, and probably much safer, to lift off into the air and fly away from the scene, but she didn't. The sudden danger resolved her deadlock, and an instant later she was running for her life behind Kevin's retreating tail and leaping for the safety of a dark hole in the side of an upturned couch. Together with several other rats they wormed their way between the springs and stuffing into the safety of the deep interior. From there they could hear the dog sniffing and scratching at the torn fabric, but they were quite confident that he couldn't reach them. Before long he became bored and gave up. The rats wasted no time. As soon as he was out of sight, they emerged again.

Suddenly, Tess found her mind full of vivid and disturbing images: an owl in the dog's mouth with feathers flying, herself as a rat being shaken in the dog's teeth, the horrifying sound and sensation of her spine snapping. She stood transfixed, trying to clear her mind, until Kevin caught hold of her by the whiskers and gave them a tweak. It was then that she remembered what he had said about rats having a visual language, and she realized that those angry images had been sent by him. Before she could work out how to answer him, they were approached by another rat and then another, and her mind was fully occupied by their expressions and the images they were passing.

"Here among us, you two, huh? Days and nights, days and nights, us lot listening, looking, huh?"

Tess was surprised at how well she understood them.

"You two sleeping, huh? Days and nights, days and nights. Stuffing fat bacon, huh? Trying to make a family, huh?"

Tess was shocked, but Kevin was angry. He jumped onto the rat who had suggested it and bit his ear until he squealed. "Ear gone, nanananana! Sit down, calm, days and nights, you two, empty streets, empty skies."

Kevin was sending images now. "Long road. Us two, many streets. Very sore feet."

Tess was grateful that he didn't let them know that the delay was largely her fault. "Many streets, many streets," she thought, "yep," and she was surprised when the others nodded and twitched their whiskers.

"Yep, yep, many streets. Many streets behind, many streets ahead, move, run, little old lady sitting beside a fire, looking you two, listening you two, run, huh?"

And run they did, straight away. Across the waste ground and down a hole which led under the foundations of the neighboring house and through a series of underground passages lined with brick, earth, and rubble.

Kevin went ahead with the rat whose ear he had bitten. The other stranger ran along beside Tess, watching her cautiously with what she interpreted as a rather stupid grin. From time to time the passageway grew narrow and the lead rat and Kevin would fall into single file until they were through. But Tess's

companion didn't seem to understand. If she gained
speed to go ahead, he gained speed as well, and if she
slowed down to drop behind, he also slowed, all the
time looking at her with that same stupid expression.
They survived a couple of tight squeezes, but managed to become completely stuck at one particularly
narrow spot.

"Oops," said her guide in rat language. "Narrow,
narrow. Us two, oooh, very, very thin, huh? Squeeze."

Tess scrabbled with her claws and they managed
after a brief struggle to break free. They ran on. It was
quite dark down there beneath the houses, and Tess
realized that she was following an unknown sense that
wasn't sight. She was aware of the spaces around her
and the way the tunnels changed ahead and behind,
even though she could actually see very little.

After a while, they emerged into the open space of
a basement, where light from a lamppost on the street
above flooded through the gates.

The rats stopped and looked around cautiously
before scuttling together across the empty space,
which seemed huge after the narrow tunnels. At the
other side they formed a line again to slip through a
hole in a corner. Kevin was ahead of Tess and as he disappeared down the hole she noticed that his right hind
foot had only three toes. But before she had a chance

to wonder about it, her companion was back along-side her.

"Long nose," he said.

"Huh?"

"Long nose."

They were approaching another tight gap, and this time Tess stopped and thought as clearly as she could of the two of them going through it quite sensibly and politely, one at a time. But to her annoyance, her guide stopped as well, and said again, "Long nose."

She made a sprint for the narrow gap, but he was too quick for her and there was no doubt that they would have got stuck again if Tess hadn't stopped in time. He grabbed hold of her whiskers and pulled her around to face him. She could just see the outline of his face in the darkness.

"Long nose," he said, and he caught hold of his own nose and pulled it. She noticed for the first time that he did have an unusually long nose.

"Long nose," she said, and was pleased to find that sarcasm was a readily available quality in the rat language. "Yep, yep. Sunny days, happy rats, long nose. Me through the hole, you through the hole behind me, huh?"

He wrinkled his nose. "Yep, yep," he said, and she darted through before he had time to change his mind.

Kevin and his friend were waiting, but ran on when they saw the other two coming.

"Long nose," said Tess's companion yet again. Tess was beginning to get really fed up. "Long nose," she said. "Small brain."

"Huh?"

Tess mimicked his grin. "Long nose happy you, happy me, huge sack of oats in a big barn with no cats."

"Nanananana. Long nose. You, huh?"

"Short nose."

"Nanana. Short-nosed rat in a hotel basement, many many streets."

At last Tess understood, and she felt slightly foolish. Long Nose was his symbol, his mark, his name in the visual language of rats.

"You, huh?" he said again.

Tess was at a loss. Her name was meaningless in this world. There was no way to translate it. And as far as she could tell, she was a very plain rat with no outstanding features at all. Her mind searched for images, but none of them seemed suitable.

"Owl, huh?" she said at last.

"Nanana," said Long Nose. "Nanananana. Owl carrying off young rats, us rats sad, us rats angry."

There was another narrow opening ahead, and this

time Tess managed successfully to communicate the idea of single file. She ran ahead of Long Nose into the dark gap and was surprised to find that it stayed dark and narrow. It was sludgy and slippery underfoot and there was a strong smell of drains. She waited for the tunnel to broaden out, but it didn't, and it soon began to seem as though it never would. Tess began to feel claustrophobic. The only reassurance was the sound of Kevin's pattering feet before her, and those of Long Nose's behind. Gradually the smell grew stronger and Tess realized that it was more than just drains. It was sewers. The stone passage they were in was sloping downward now, and Tess found herself beginning to slither on the slimy stuff beneath her feet.

"This is the most foolish thing I've ever done," she thought to herself. "What on earth am I doing here? How could I have allowed myself to be talked into this?"

She had no time to dwell on it, however, because the next moment Kevin flashed her an image of a rat wearing a parachute, and then they were falling through the air in the darkness.

# chapter eight

chapter eight

They landed with a splash, a shock of cold water that made Tess gasp and splutter. But before she knew it she was swimming, and quite strongly, too. For someone who had never tried to swim before, either as a girl or any other creature, it was pretty exciting and completely took her mind off the nature of the liquid they were traveling in.

There was just enough light for her to see the shapes of the other rats ahead of her and she swam up close beside Kevin before Long Nose had a chance to move in and monopolize her again.

Kevin looked across and acknowledged her with a brief nod. His eyes sparkled and she caught the image he gave her of an underground train speeding along beneath a huge city. Then he sent her a second one, of four rats going twice as fast through their own underground system. If she had known how, she would have laughed.

Before long, the four of them came to a wider canal. They swam with a gentle current until they came to a shoal of stones and sludge and trapped paper, which allowed them to climb out of the water and into another system of pipes and drains.

Tess was beginning to get tired. The drains seemed to go on forever, always sloping gently upward and always wet and slimy underfoot. It took all her strength and concentration to keep close to Kevin, who seemed to find the going no problem, and the whole business was made worse by the irritating presence of Long Nose, who trod on her tail at every possible opportunity.

She called in Rat to Kevin, "Boy and girl, out in the open, deep breaths, sleeping."

He called back, "Boy and girl squashed in drainpipe. Spaghetti." By the time they emerged, quite suddenly, into the cold, clear air, Tess was so exhausted that she felt she couldn't travel another yard. She wanted badly to be human, at least for a while, but before she could repeat her request to Kevin they were off again. They had come out onto another piece of waste ground that lay between two huge warehouses. Tess followed the others out onto a wide street. There was no sign of people or dogs, but they stuck to the deepest shadows all the same, running in single file close up to the walls and sprinting across the open spaces in between. At the end of the street lay the river. Ships were tied up beneath cranes, waiting for loading or unloading, but there was no activity now. All was still and silent.

The fresh air had given Tess a second wind and she was comfortable enough now as the little group followed the warehouse walls parallel to the river for several hundred yards. There were lights here, and they were much more exposed to possible danger than they had been in the drains, but Tess was happier. The others, however, did not relax until they left the warehouses behind them and crossed through the chain-link fence that surrounded an area of huge coal heaps. Then they slowed their pace and picked their way among the loose slag at leisure.

"Dawn," said Kevin, dropping back beside Tess.

"Happy us," said Tess. "Boy, girl, sitting on the coal, huh? Boy smoking cigarette, huh? Talking, huh?"

"Us four sleeping," said Kevin. "Curled together, warm."

It was not an image that appealed to Tess, though it clearly did to him. She was still not entirely comfortable about being a rat and, besides that, it would be the first time that she had allowed herself to sleep as an animal. It was an idea that had always scared her a little, not only because she might sleep longer than she meant to and arrive home late, but because sleeping was a kind of forgetting and she was afraid that she might not remember who she was when she woke up.

Kevin nudged her with his shoulder and wrinkled his nose. Then he darted on ahead and, resigning herself, Tess followed.

The four rats slept throughout the day in a snug and well-concealed hole beneath an entrance to a coal yard. It was far from being a sound sleep. The floor above their heads was walked on almost constantly, and the sounds of men's voices filtered through. Trucks passed in and out all day, their tires crunching on the coal dust.

But Tess didn't mind. Rat dreams were strange and frightening and it was a relief to be awakened from time to time and remember where she was and why. Sometimes Kevin woke with her and they would exchange a few images and touch noses for comfort before they went back to sleep. Sometimes the rat with the bitten ear woke and moved in small, irritated circles, trying to get comfortable again. Long Nose didn't wake at all but snored and sighed throughout all the coming and going in ignorant contentment.

The best sleep came in the three or four hours between the closing of the coal yard and the arrival of darkness. Those hours passed like minutes but refreshed the four rats better than any before them. When they woke, they spent a few minutes cleaning themselves, then emerged, bright-eyed and sleek, into the strange orange gloom that covers cities at night. A few flakes of snow were falling but there was little wind, and the rats were in no danger of getting cold as long as they kept moving. They were hungry, though, and Tess discovered that the hunger of a rat bore no relation to any hunger she had ever known. It began as a warm and rather pleasant sensation that made her feel energetic and strong. Within an hour it had grown larger and more demanding, and she felt enormous courage and pride. She was sure that she could steal a bone from a dog and she longed for a chance to prove it.

"Eat, huh?" she blasted at Kevin.

He jumped at the force of her message but answered calmly: "Basement, dark, black bags, good restaurant, a few streets."

Tess held on to the image of the diners in their expensive clothes, taking their time over their food. Her parents took her to that kind of place from time to time, but she was sure that Kevin would never have been in one, at least not while he was human. Tess decided she would invite him out when all this was over. She had her own money, quite a bit in a savings account, and she would buy him some new clothes if he would let her. It was a pleasant fantasy. She would be on familiar territory. He would be on edge, worse than usual, but she'd make him feel at ease and make sure he got the best the restaurant had to offer.

"Long Nose."

Not again. Tess almost squeaked in annoyance. She was tempted to use the pent-up urgency of her hunger to jump on him and box his ears, but just in time she realized that he was probably hungry, too. By now they were back among the rat runs that honey-comb the foundations of the city, and Tess had allowed herself to fall back behind Kevin again and into the company of Long Nose.

"You, huh?" he said.

Tess was as stuck as before. To make time, she said: "Him, huh?" and sent an image of the rat with the chewed ear.

"One black whisker."

Tess hadn't noticed. "Him, huh?" she said, indicating Kevin.

The image that came back was a disturbing one, an awful random mixture of rat features combined with the rat's version of what a boy is. Tess had no desire to have a name-image anything like that.

"You, huh?" said Long Nose again.

Tess said nothing.

"Huh? Huh?"

When she still made no reply, he gave her a command that no rat will ever refuse, because too often their lives depend upon it.

"Freeze!" Tess froze. But Long Nose did not. He walked all around her from her nose to her tail, muttering to himself. "Huh? Huh? Nananana. Nope. Huh?"

He tugged at her tail and her whiskers, prodded her nose and looked into her ears. He lifted her feet and counted her teeth and made her sit up while he examined her belly, all the while saying: "Huh? Nope. Nananana. Nope." At last he went around behind her and seemed to be measuring her tail again. "Tail two toes short, huh?" he said.

Tess didn't catch the image. "Huh?" she said. "Three toes, four toes, huh?" he asked.

"Huh?" She turned around to see what he was doing, just as he bit off the last inch and a half of her tail.

Tess squeaked and swung around ready to attack, but Long Nose looked amazed and offered his throat in defense.

"Hurt!" she said. "Tail, yowch!"

"Seven toes," said Long Nose, holding up the end of her tail and measuring it against his front paw. "You, Tail Short Seven Toes."

Tess examined the wound on her tail and was surprised to see that it was hardly bleeding at all. Nor was it anywhere near as sore as she expected it to be. She could live with it, she decided, and would almost have forgiven Long Nose had she not turned around to find him contentedly eating the end of her tail for his breakfast. She sent him an insult that even he could not fail to understand, and ran ahead to find Kevin.

The rats feasted on the garbage in the basement of the restaurant. There were other rats there, too, pleased to meet the newcomers and exchange the latest gossip. One of them, a handsome fellow who introduced himself to Tess as "Stuck Six Days in a Gutter Pipe," showed her how to recognize rat poison and scatter bits of it around to make it look as if it had been eaten. Then he helped her to find the choicest bits of leftover food, such as fish spines, chicken hearts, and slivers of soap. Tess accepted them as graciously as her rat nature permitted, but it seemed to her with her great hunger that anything she ate was as good as the next thing, and that was even better.

There was plenty for everyone and the place seemed to have a constant turnover of rodent customers who came and went in a leisurely fashion. Stuck Six Days in a Gutter Pipe wrinkled his nose suavely at Tess as he left, but the effect was slightly spoiled by the chicken leg in his mouth that he was taking home for his children.

When Tess had eaten all she could, she joined Kevin and One Black Whisker in a quiet corner where they were chatting with two unknown rats.

"Guides," Kevin told her. "Long Nose, One Black Whisker curled up asleep in the couch on the waste ground. Little old woman sitting beside a fire, many streets. Long Nose and One Black Whisker confused, lost."

"Many streets, huh?" said Tess. "Boy, girl walking, riding on a bus. Owls, pigeons flying. Us rats going slowly. Us rats very tired. Us rats sleeping."

"Boy, girl scratching their heads," said Kevin. "Looking at maps shrugging their shoulders."

"Us rats swimming in sewers, us rats in slimy black drainpipes."

"Girl going into her house, huh?" Kevin's black eyes were cold and mistrustful and Tess knew her own must have looked the same. But he was right. There was no turning back now, and no way of knowing where to go without the guidance of the city rats. She showed Kevin her teeth for spite, but a few minutes later they were back on the rat highways with their new guides.

c h a p t e r   n i n e

For three more nights Tess and Kevin traveled through the rats' city underground, changing guides twice more along the way. They ate from trash cans knocked over by dogs, from supermarket storage bins and from the shelves of poorly guarded kitchens. When they reached the outskirts of the city they began to travel above the ground, and they stopped many times along the way in urban gardens to feed on tasty scraps from compost heaps. Rats, it seemed, were never short of food.

On the fourth day, dawn found them in one of the most affluent areas of the country. Green fields and trees surrounded impressive houses, both old and new, owned by those people who could afford the luxury of having the best of both worlds. Tess was aware that her parents had checked out areas like this before they settled on the house beside the park. The air was so fresh and the country smells so sweet that she found herself regretting their choice. What was puzzling her, though, was that the sort of area they were in didn't fit at all with the picture the rats had given her of the little old lady who was waiting beside the fire.

"Little old lady, huh?" she said to their latest guide. Her name was Nose Broken by a Mousetrap, and it was easy to see why.

"Yep, yep, little old lady," she said, and darted through a hedge into a field of lush grass.

It was not snowing now, but there had been several light snowfalls over the last few days, and because of the relentless cold, whatever snow had settled had remained. It stuck to the rats now as they dislodged it from the grass, and melted in dark patches on their glossy coats. They stayed close in to the hedge to avoid the eyes of dogs or hawks or passersby, and soon they crossed into a second meadow, and then a third. A road ran parallel to their route, between the meadows and the widely spaced houses on the opposite side, and the occasional car passed along it, driving slowly because of the icy conditions. After a while, Tess realized by the change that the hedge they were following was no longer beside the road but running away from it and out into the open country.

"Road, huh?" she said. "Little old lady house, huh?"

"Yep, yep," said Nose Broken by a Mousetrap, and she led the way through the twisted roots of the hedge. They stopped on the other side. They were on the edge of a green path with high, brambly hedges on each side. Blackthorn and ash trees grew overhead and almost made a tunnel. It was a path for people and animals only, far too narrow for a car.

"House," said Nose Broken by a Mousetrap, pointing with her nose along the path.

"House, huh?" said Kevin.

"House, yep. Little old lady. Yep, yep. Careful. Cats. Many cats. Follow drainage pipe. Passage through hollow walls, comes out above the fireplace. Cats can't reach." She touched noses with each of them and said, "Nose Broken by a Mousetrap visiting her grandchildren. No hair yet. Many streets." And with that she was gone, back through the hedge and out of their lives.

"House," said Kevin, and started running down the path. But this time Tess didn't follow.

"Freeze!" she said.

He did, instantly. Tess looked up and down the path. She sniffed the air and listened carefully for a while. They were well hidden from the road by a curve in the path, and the hedges were high on either side. With a sigh of relief, she switched into human form, and after a moment or two Kevin did the same.

Tess arched her back, stretched her arms above

her head, and then swung them around like a wind-mill, all those things that a rat can't do. Then she sighed again and sat down against the base of a tree where the ground was free from snow.

"Shove up," said Kevin.

Tess moved over, turning away from him, and he squeezed in beside her with his back against hers. "What did you do that for?" he said.

"Do what?"

"Change"

"We're going to see a little old lady, aren't we?"

"Yes. But she obviously speaks Rat, doesn't she? How else could she have sent the others looking for us, huh?"

"Don't 'huh?' me," snapped Tess. "I'm fed up with being a rat. That wasn't part of the deal as far as I'm concerned. It's all right for you. You're used to it. Maybe too used to it."

"Oh," said Kevin, "like that, is it? Well, maybe you're too used to being a rotten human. We didn't make the stinking sewers and slimy drainpipes, you know? You did. We don't leave garbage thrown around all over the place. It's your lot who does that. You're lucky you've got us to clean up after you!"

Tess was staring at him, openmouthed.

"What's wrong?" he said.

"What do you mean, 'us'?"

Kevin looked at the ground and gathered a small lump of snow in his hand.

"What do you mean, Kevin?" Tess went on. "What are you trying to say?"

"Nothing," he said. "It's just that I'm not good at being a boy. With rats you know where you stand even if it isn't always pleasant. But I don't understand people properly. They say one thing and they mean another. I don't know how to look at them and I don't understand the way they look at me."

Tess looked around her. A weak morning sun was pouring yellow light through the branches and picking out specks of brilliance in the thin snow. Above their heads the birds were chatting quietly, not too concerned by their presence but aware of it all the same.

"I don't either, Kevin," she said, gently. "I'm not sure anybody does. That's just the way people are."

"That's fair enough, I suppose." he said, "But it doesn't give me a good reason to bother with them."

"You keep saying 'them,' or 'you,' as if you don't belong. But you do. You're the same as any of us when it comes down to it."

"Am I, Tess?"

"Of course you are! We're all the same underneath."

Kevin sighed deeply and tilted back his head so

that it rested, just for an instant, against hers.

They walked together down the path until the house came into view. It was a tiny place and quite ancient, completely at odds with the surrounding wealth and grandeur. A few hens pecked at the grass around the front door, and a troop of ducks that were puddling around in the mud beside an outside tap took offense at the presence of strangers and waddled away in a line, quacking contemptuously.

The little old lady heard them and came to the door.

"At last," she said. "I thought you'd never get here, so I did."

"Pardon?" said Tess.

"I been waiting ages," said the little old lady. "You took your time, didn't you?" She threw a suspicious glance at Kevin and said, "I thought you was a rat."

Kevin looked crestfallen and hung behind Tess as they followed the old woman into the house.

"Never mind," she said, pushing cats off chairs beside the fire to make room for them to sit down. "I suppose you is a rat and you isn't. It's all the same in the end. All the same to me at any rate. Sit yourselves down, and don't take any notice of them cats. A knee is a knee to a cat and a lap is a lap, and whether it's a knee or a lap it's warmer than the floor. If you doesn't like cats," she looked pointedly at Kevin, "you can tell them where to get off, but politely, mind, because we doesn't tolerate rudeness in this house, does we pussums, eh?"

She closed the hall door behind them and they settled, a little self-consciously, into the newly vacated chairs. The fire was crackling brightly and a large black kettle on a hook above it was wheezing in a way that made Tess hope for tea. It seemed like a year since she had tasted it.

As soon as the old woman sat down the cats began to gather on her lap, and before long there were four of them there, maneuvering for position.

"Tell us your names," said the old woman. "Come on, don't be shy."

The cats sat gazing out at Tess and Kevin with narrow, malevolent eyes. Kevin was looking pointedly at the floor and Tess knew that he wasn't going to be any help at all.

"Well," she said, "he's Kevin and I'm Tess."

"Oh," said the old woman. "Kevin, is he? That's a good, solid name, now, Kevin is. You can't argue with that, can you?

"I suppose not," said Tess.

"But Tess," the old woman went on, without pausing for breath, "isn't a name at all. It's one of those ridiculous new inventions like a sticky label. They might as well have given you a number, miss, as a name like that."

"But that's not true!" said Tess, beginning to get annoyed. "It's a very old name."

"A very old name? How can it be a very old name when you's only a little nipper, eh? I'll tell you a very old name. Lizzie is a very old name, and I isn't telling you how old it is, and as every young gentleman knows," she leaned forward and poked Kevin on the knee so that he jumped, "it isn't polite to ask. But you can take it from me, it's a very old name. It's very nearly about as old a name as you can get."

There was an awkward silence, during which the kettle's voice moved up a semitone. Tess glanced around the room surreptitiously. Beside the fireplace was an old black oven, and above it Tess noticed a hole in the stonework of the chimney front which she recognized from Nose Broken by a Mousetrap's description. She could well imagine Lizzie sitting there in the evenings, having conversations with little twitching noses poking out, while the cats prowled below in impotent fury.

Behind them was a small table, and beyond that an old-fashioned square sink between cupboards with broken doors. There was a litter of bits and pieces everywhere, but Tess had the impression that, on the whole, the place was clean. Light streamed in from a large window behind the sink. Tess took a second look, unable to believe what she had seen. Hanging on a line above the window, like an eccentric pelmet, were a half dozen pairs of Lizzie's drawers.

Tess looked at Kevin, but he was picking imaginary dirt from beneath his fingernails. It was clear that the old woman was rubbing him the wrong way.

"Is Lizzie your name, then?" she said, still battling with the giggles that were threatening to erupt.

"It isn't what I'd have chosen if I was given the choice," said the old woman, "but we never is, is we? There it is, as soon as we's big enough to know it, and then we's stuck with it, isn't we? We can't shake it off, can we pussums, eh? Born Lizzie I was, and Lizzie I'll be to the end of my days if there ever is an end to them."

Tess realized that Kevin was swearing silently, in Rat.

"You has a very lazy tongue, young man," said Lizzie, "but a nasty, busy little mind. And you's very stupid if you thinks I can't know what you's saying."

Kevin looked up, shocked. "Sorry," he said. "I forgot."

"You forgot, so you did," said Lizzie. "Teenagers

always forgets. Teenagers thinks they's the only ones with eyes and the only ones with brains. I was a rat, young Kevin, before your father had an eye to have a gleam in. I was a rat in the days when those things wasn't done, and many other things besides. I was a rat in days when teenagers wasn't allowed. What do you think of that, eh?"

Kevin looked daggers at Tess and she glared back at him. It hadn't been her idea to come here. It was becoming clear to her that the old woman was mad as a hatter. Her parents would be at home, out of their minds with worry, and she had spent four nights in the sewers of Dublin to come and listen to total nonsense.

Lizzie put the cats down off her knee, one by one, and got up. She reached out and gave the kettle a prod so that it swayed on its hook and hissed angrily. "Get a move on," she said to it. "You's always slow when I's in a hurry. You does it on purpose."

The hissing died down and a few weak puffs of steam escaped from the spout. "These days," Lizzie went on, "anything goes, doesn't it, eh pussums? Anyone who wants to can be a teenager. You sees them everywhere with their hair all painted and their raggedy clothes and every one of them knows better than the next one. Oh, it's an awful thing. Dreadful.

It's catching, too. It's an epidemic. And some people is never cured, never. Some people is teenagers all their lives. Isn't that right, pussums?"

Kevin stood up and turned to Tess. "I've had enough of this," he said.

"Oh?" said Lizzie, putting her hands on her hips. "Had enough, has you? You hasn't had anything yet, so how is it you's had enough? If you's had enough, why did you come at all?"

"Come on, Tess," said Kevin. Tess stood up a little uncertainly, looking from one to the other.

"That's teenagers for you," Lizzie went on, her voice rising in tone to near hysteria. "They hasn't even started and they's had enough. They only wants to sit in front of the TV or have a good time for theirselves being jackdaws and puppies and toads. They's always had enough, even before they's had what they come for!"

Kevin wheeled on her, and the cats, which had occupied her vacated chair, scattered in all directions. "And what about stupid old women? Who invites . . . who invite people to visit them and drag them across Dublin and then tell them to mind their manners so they can stand there and abuse them?"

"You hasn't any manners to mind!" shouted Lizzie.

"Listen to who's talking!" yelled Kevin, and he stormed out. He was halfway up the little path before

Tess caught up with him. She was very relieved that he hadn't switched, because she would have had a lot of difficulty finding a rat, and as for a pigeon or a hawk, it would have been hopeless. The fact that he hadn't meant that there was still a chance.

"Wait, Kevin," she said.

"What for?"

"I want to talk to you for a minute."

"Talk?" he said. "That's all people ever do. Talk, talk, talk. They talk so much they get on each other's nerves and what happens then? They have to bloody well talk about it!"

"Don't be like that, Kevin."

"Why not? What's the point of all that talking, eh? Now you want to talk about that stupid old woman, and we wouldn't be here in the first place if it weren't for her talking too much."

"Will you just listen for a minute?"

Kevin sighed and turned to face her. His eyes were grim and determined, and her heart sank. He could disappear so easily, just vanish from her life into the skies or the underground passages of the city and she would never be able to find him again.

"Don't you see?" she said. "The old woman is like you. She doesn't understand people, either. She doesn't know how to behave."

Kevin looked away from her. "It just proves my point, doesn't it?" he said. "It's a waste of time trying to understand people." But Tess knew that he was disarmed now.

"Maybe you're right," she said. "Maybe it will all turn out to be a wild goose chase. But we can't just give up without finding out. We have to hear what she has to say." Kevin looked at her again, and she could see that his anger was dissolving. Tess looked back toward the house.

"Do you know something, Kevin?" she said.

"What?"

"You care a lot more about people than you think you do."

"Oh, do I?" His voice was full of contempt. "Why do you think that?"

"Because if you really didn't care, if you really thought people were so useless, then they couldn't upset you, could they? Because you'd never expect anything better."

Kevin didn't answer, but looked at Tess suspiciously. She began to walk back down the path toward the house and after a while he followed.

c h a p t e r   t e n

At that moment, in the United Nations Building, a meeting of the Security Council was taking place. Representatives from all the member countries in the Northern Hemisphere were present. The meeting had been in progress for some time and Captain Miller and General Barker's two tapes had been played, and then played again. The mood was somber.

"Maybe those young men in the snowmobile just woke up a polar bear or something," said the Finnish delegate.

No one ventured to answer. In light of what they had just heard, the question seemed to answer itself. After a while, he continued. "Well, what are we supposed to think? That there are some kind of aliens up there or something?"

Again no one answered. Quite a few of those present had already come to the unpleasant conclusion that there was no other explanation.

At length, the chairperson of the Intergovernmental Panel on Climate Change spoke. "Our recommendation is twofold. We need planes above those storms and planes down in the middle of them, taking pictures with radar and infrared and every other technology we have at our disposal." There was a pause, and then, reluctantly, she went on, "In view of what we have just heard, we also recommend that the planes be fully armed and prepared to strike."

Lizzie was delighted to see Tess and Kevin return, though she did her best to hide it.

"Here they are again, pussums," she said as she opened the door. "You just never knows, does you? Forgot your tea, did you? Never mind, kettle's nearly boiling." She poked it again and it swayed and spat water onto the fire where it fizzed and steamed.

"Find your chairs, find your chairs, they's still there, no cats back in them yet. Make yourselves comfortable while I makes the tea. Come in, Oedipus, before you gets shut out." She closed the hall door firmly behind a black tomcat and leaned on it for an instant, smiling at Tess and Kevin as brightly as she could manage. Then she fell into such a frenzy of activity that it made Tess nervous to watch her.

"Where's the milk, eh? Has you had it, Moppet? No, no, that's yesterday's milk. Where did I put it now, I wonder? Well, there's not many places it can be. Oops, kettle's boiling, let's just get these tea leaves out into the garden. Does you know that, Tessie?"

"What?"

"Tea leaves is good for the garden. Nothing better. Straight out the window onto the grass they goes and the hens scratches them into the ground. Nothing better. I never puts no manure on that grass out there and there's no greener grass in the country."

There was nothing Tess hated more than being called Tessie, but she bit her tongue and said nothing.

"Warm up the teapot, now," Lizzie went on. "Have to warm the teapot, does you know that, eh? Does you warm the teapot? Takes all the good out of the tea if the teapot isn't warm. I never gets a decent cup of tea anywhere except in my own house. All these teenagers, see? They never does anything properly. They hasn't any patience."

Kevin was looking steadfastly down at the floor between his feet.

"Not yourselves, of course, yourselves is different," she added, hastily. "Now. Where's the milk?" She paused for a moment and looked around, as though not quite sure where she was. Then her pale blue eyes brightened. "I suppose it's still out in the pantry. Of course it is. It's cooling down, that's what it's doing.

Don't go away now, little Switchers. I'll be back in a second."

Tess nudged Kevin's shoulder. He looked up sternly, then dropped his guard and smiled. Lizzie came back and bumbled around in cupboards for a while, collecting an assortment of chipped cups and odd saucers. At last, after what seemed an age, she handed them each a piping hot cup of tea and sat down in a chair with her own.

Kevin seemed to approve of the tea. He sat back in his chair and sipped it slowly. "Very good," he said to Lizzie.

"Ah!" she said. "You speaks then? I wasn't sure. I wasn't sure at all." It was the worst thing she could have said. Kevin scowled and retreated into sullen silence. Tess took a deep breath.

"I suppose we'd better get down to business," she said.

"Business?" said Lizzie. "What business? I can't stand business. Never has anything to do with it. All them fields out there is mine, you know, and there's a track worn to my door with business people coming to try and buy them off me. What does they want with them, says I? I never seen a farmer in a suit like they wears." She laughed suddenly, long and loud. "I tells them to take their business back where they came from and keep it out of my fields."

"But they must be worth a fortune!" said Kevin. "Why don't you sell them?"

"What does I want with a fortune?" said Lizzie. "I has a fortune already. I has a house of my own and my cats and hens and ducks and my Nancy. I has green fields all around me and I likes it that way. I lets a farmer use the land and he brings me everything I needs from the shops. What's that if it isn't a fortune?"

"But you could live anywhere. Have anything you want," said Kevin.

"I lives somewhere already, and I has everything I wants." For a moment all three of them were silent, and then Lizzie looked at Kevin and said, "Now I knows you isn't a rat."

Kevin clicked his tongue and sighed in exasperation. Tess sniffed the tea and had a nasty suspicion that she knew who and what Nancy was, but she decided to ignore it and think of more important things. "I didn't really mean *that* kind of business," she said. "I meant the business of why we're here. Why you told the rats to bring us here."

"Oh," said Lizzie. "That's something different altogether, isn't it? That's not business. That's a matter of altogether more urgency, that is."

"Right," said Tess, gently. "Then perhaps it'd be a good idea if we talked about it."

"Oh, not now," said Lizzie. "No, that would never do."

"But you just said it was urgent," said Kevin.

"There's some things in life," said Lizzie, "that just can't be talked about when the sun is shining and the birds are singing. There's some things that aren't fit to be seen, or heard, or said, or even thought in the daytime, no matter how urgent they is." She threw Kevin a disdainful glance. "If you was a rat, you'd know that."

Kevin got to his feet in exasperation and stuffed his hands into the pockets of his jeans. "Then I'm going out for a walk," he said.

"Hold on," said Lizzie. "We'll all go in a few minutes, and you can meet Nancy. But let's have another cup of tea first. After all, it isn't every day I has a couple of young Switchers to visit me."

# chapter eleven

chapter eleven

When Tess and Kevin had finished their second cup of tea, Lizzie took them out to the back of the cottage to meet Nancy. She was a white goat, as Tess had suspected, and she was tethered by a long rope in a scrubby field that lay between the orchard and the ruins of what was once a large and rather grand house.

"I lived there once," said Lizzie, "many years ago. But it was too big for me all on my own. I prefers the cottage."

Nancy stayed where she was as the three of them approached, and chewed her cud with weary patience as Lizzie prattled over her. Tess had something of the same distaste for goats that she had for rats. They were the poor relations of the other farmyard animals, always bony, always hungry, always eating what they shouldn't.

"There now, Nancy," Lizzie was saying. "Isn't you a lovely goat? You's the best little goat in the world, so you is. You's my poppet. This here is Kevin, and this one here is Tessie. They's Switchers, both of them."

Nancy spotted a few green bramble leaves that she had missed earlier in the day and barged her way between her admirers to collect them. Lizzie looked a bit embarrassed. "She's very fond of me, really," she said. "But she's shy of strangers. Was you ever a goat?"

Kevin nodded, but Tess shook her head.

"Really, Tess?" said Kevin. "Were you *never?*"

"No."

"But why not?"

"Oh, I don't know. I never fancied it I suppose."

"Goats is all right," said Lizzie, "except that they has poor manners. Not Nancy, of course. Nancy has manners."

But Nancy wasn't there to display them. She had disappeared around the other side of a clump of brambles and was straining as hard as she could on her tether.

"They has brains, though," Lizzie went on. "Goats has wonderful brains. Ten times as many as sheep has."

"It's true, Tess," said Kevin. "Why don't you try it, eh? We could go for a spin."

"You can't do that," said Lizzie. "That's bad manners. You's only just arrived."

"But we wouldn't be long. Just a quick spin." Kevin turned toward Tess so that Lizzie couldn't see his face, then he widened his eyes in a pleading way, and Tess realized that she was being very slow. He wanted an excuse to get away from the old woman for a while.

"Oh," she said, "all right. I suppose it could be interesting."

"Now I thinks about it," said Lizzie, "it's not such a bad idea. You two could do me a favor."

"How?" said Kevin, slightly suspicious.

"Easy. There's a few gardens around here that could do with a bit of a trim by a pair of goats, specially those ones up the road. They sneers at me if I's out for a stroll. They thinks they's better than me what with all their fancy cars and posh clothes and their business and all."

Kevin looked at Tess with mischief shining in his eyes. "Come on. What are you waiting for?"

Tess hesitated, thinking of her own mother and her love for each of her gardens, wherever she lived. And her father had a fancy car and good suits and worked in what Lizzie scornfully referred to as "business." If they had bought a house here instead of near the park, it might have been her own garden they were intending to "trim." She looked at Kevin. He was waiting eagerly for her reply. They were living on opposite sides of the tracks, she realized. And yet, they were alike.

"You thinks about things too much, young lady," said Lizzie.

"That's true," said Kevin. "She's right for once."

"You bad-mannered little pup!" said Lizzie. "Go on, the two of you. Get out of here and eat some shrubs while you still has the chance."

Kevin winked at Tess and looked around. They were well hidden, there among the bushes and trees. "Make sure you isn't white, now, whatever else you does," said Lizzie. "I don't want anyone coming blaming my Nancy."

Tess was convinced. While Lizzie watched, they made their change. Nancy stared around the edge of the bushes, astonished by the sudden appearance of two goats, one brown and one black.

"Ooh," said Lizzie. "That did me the power of good, that did. Makes me feel young again."

But none of the three goats understood a word that she said.

Tess and Kevin hopped over the stone wall that bounded the scrubby field and into a small orchard. Behind them they could hear Nancy bleating pathetically at the loss of her new friends. For a moment or two they hesitated, drawn quite strongly by the call of one of their own kind, but then they moved off among the trees, browsing on the leaves and twigs that were within their reach. There were windfalls lying on the ground, apples and pears, but they were small and hard and bitter because of the long spell of cold. The leaves had suffered, too, and those that had not already fallen were fibrous and dry, but to a goat they were as delicious as mature cheese.

Tess was surprised by some of the things that she was learning. She found that it was a myth that goats would eat anything. On the contrary, her senses of smell and taste were so refined that she could tell in an instant whether a moth had laid eggs on a leaf or a bird dropping had landed there, even a month ago. She would leave anything that was the slightest bit tainted where it was on the tree, and eat carefully around it. She found that she had a rich and rare sense of her own independence, and that as much as she enjoyed the pleasure of Kevin's company, she would depart from him without hesitation if the need arose. Nancy was still bleating on the other side of the hedge, and although Tess recognized that the sound held within it the desire for company, she knew that Nancy was calling for more than that. For stronger than every other emotion in a goat's heart is the love of freedom. Even here, amid the luxury of the rich lands where food would never be scarce, her goat soul longed for the high, craggy places of the world, places that are of no use to mankind but are the wild, windy kingdoms of the goats.

Tess and Kevin browsed their way peacefully to the edge of the orchard where two strands of barbed wire reinforced a neglected hedge. On the other side of it, cattle were grazing.

Kevin turned to Tess, and the sly, mischievous glint was in his eye again. Tess knew that for the first time, she was returning it. Together they slipped through the fence as if it wasn't there and strolled out into the field.

The cattle stared, disconcerted, and swung to face them, blowing blasts of steaming air from their nostrils. For the hell of it, Kevin jumped at them, and they spun on their heels with surprising speed and careered away across the field. A goat can't laugh, but Tess's heart stretched with mirth as she watched them. Stupid creatures.

From where she and Kevin stood, they could see the neatly trimmed hedges of the nearest house, and with another quick glance of agreement, they set out toward it. Behind them the cattle followed cautiously, closely grouped for safety.

The two goats squeezed under the barbed wire at the edge of the field and found themselves outside a large, neat garden. It was surrounded by a stone wall with a wide coping stone running along the top. The wall was high enough to deter a stray cow or sheep, and more than high enough to contain the little terrier who yapped at them from the other side. He was one of those pampered little dogs that are never found in farmyards or houses that have children, and he had never in his life encountered rough treatment. To protect him against the cold, he wore a red tartan jacket that made him feel a lot bigger and stronger than he should have.

Kevin hopped effortlessly onto the top of the wall, and Tess joined him. The little dog began to yap hysterically, halfway between the garden wall and the safety of the house, halfway between rage and terror. Inside the house, his mistress turned up the volume on the TV to cover the noise he was making. More often than not, he turned out to be yapping at nothing.

Kevin jumped down into the garden without warning and ran full tilt at the dog, who paused for an instant in astonishment, then ran yelping around the side of the house. When Kevin gave up the chase and returned to nibble the top off a young Japanese willow, the terrier took up a position at a corner of the house and stood there watching with his tail between his legs.

The hours passed. Lizzie busied herself around the house and garden and waited for her visitors to return. Around mid-afternoon she hacked a couple of parsnips out of the frozen ground of her garden, and collected carrots and a turnip from the potting shed where they were stored in boxes of sand.

"They shouldn't be hungry by the time they gets back," she said to Nancy, "but in my experience them teenagers always is, no matter how much you gives them."

She brought the vegetables into the kitchen and ran water in the sink. Outside the window the sky had clouded over, and as she stood there wondering if it was going to start snowing she saw a policeman coming down the path.

"Watch out, pussums," she said. "You'd better make yourselves scarce. Here comes trouble."

# chapter twelve

"Hello?" called the policeman. "Anybody home?"

Lizzie went over to the window, where she made a big show of peering around the folds of the curtain. The policeman saw her, smiled, and lifted his cap.

"Who is it?" said Lizzie.

"No need to be afraid," said the policeman. "I'd just like a word with you for a minute. Can I come in? It's awful cold out here."

Lizzie went into the hallway, where she tidied up a pile of newspapers and rearranged the coats on their pegs. There was another knock.

"All right" said Lizzie impatiently. "I's coming."

At last she opened the door. The policeman started to come inside, but Lizzie stood solidly in the doorway and didn't move. He sighed. "Garda John Maloney," he said. "I believe you're known as Lizzie."

"That's right, yes." Lizzie nodded.

"Are you by any chance missing two goats?" asked the policeman.

"Goats?" said Lizzie. "I hasn't got two goats, so how could I be missing them?"

"I see. Your neighbors led us to believe that you kept goats," said Garda John Maloney.

"I has one goat," said Lizzie firmly. "Just one. Her name is Nancy and she's tied up out in the brambles where she always is. Who told you I keeps goats? If anyone has any complaints about Nancy they can bring them to me theirselves or else keep their mouths shut. Nancy has better manners than the rest of that lot put together."

"No, no," said the garda. "It's nothing like that. It's just that we've got rather a problem, you see."

Tess and Kevin, communicating by a combination of goat gestures and rat images, were having a ball. Three policemen and a gathering of neighborhood residents were red in the face with exertion and fury. The goats dodged and scrambled, jumped walls, and pushed through hedges. They split up without hesitation when they had to and met again as soon as they could. They avoided traps with uncanny and infuriating ease.

A local farmer had been called in to help and he had arrived full of cool confidence with his two best sheepdogs. But ten minutes after he arrived, the farmer was coaxing the terrified creatures back into his Land Rover and wondering if they would ever work again.

Few dogs are a match for a full-grown goat, and a dog that has worked all its life with timid, flock-minded sheep is particularly helpless when it finds itself suddenly looking into the unflinching yellow eyes of one of their brazen cousins.

Garda Maloney rejoined the others, leaving Lizzie to continue making her stew. It was simmering nicely when she heard the two goats returning, their hooves clattering on the frozen ground as they came careering down her path. They swung at full speed into the yard at the side of the house and veered in through the open door of the woodshed. A few seconds later, Tess and Kevin emerged laughing, their eyes still shining with mischief. They had barely gotten inside the door of the house when Garda Maloney and two local residents came running down the path. They stopped outside the front door, panting hard.

Lizzie got up from her chair and threw open the window. "Clear off!" she said. "We got no goats in here."

"But we know they're around here now, ma'am," said Garda Maloney. "We followed them down your path."

"Well, they isn't here now, and we wants to have our dinner in peace. So clear off."

Garda Maloney restrained his rising temper with some difficulty. "I'm sorry, ma'am," he said, "but those two goats have been causing havoc."

"Have you got a search warrant?" asked Lizzie, and before there was time for an answer she shut the window and turned her back on it.

"Come on, Lizzie," said Tess. "Why don't you let them look? They won't find anything."

"I don't want them poking around in my sheds and my garden, that's why. And I wants to have my dinner."

"We'll show them around, then, Kevin and I. We'll make sure they don't go poking around. Okay, Kevin?"

"Not me," said Kevin. "I don't like cops. You show them around if you like."

"Right then, I will."

Tess went out and opened the front door to the three men. They had started out toward the yard, and it was clear that they intended to have a look around, whatever Lizzie might say. Tess joined them. "I'll show you around the place," she said.

Garda Maloney smiled pleasantly and said, "Very good of you," but he looked at her just a little too long. All at once, Tess's blood ran cold. What a fool she was, what a complete and utter fool. Of course her parents would have told the police that she was missing, no matter what she had said in her note to them. She turned away and tried to collect her thoughts. "Where do you want to look first?" she said.

"Everywhere," said one of the neighbors. "We'll start in here." He looked into the woodshed, and his friend, who was tall and thin and dressed in a ridiculous one-piece down ski suit, peered in over his shoulder. Garda Maloney, however, seemed more interested in Tess. "Are you a relative of the old bird, then?" he asked.

"She's not an old bird," said Tess, thinking like a rat, thinking like a goat, wishing that she knew how to think like a fox. "She's my aunt Lizzie. My great-aunt, actually."

"Ah," said Maloney.

Tess led the way toward the henhouse. The hens were gathered around the trough, pecking at the last crumbs of their mash.

The policeman watched them absently. "Just down for the day are you?"

"Yes. My father will be here later to pick us up."

"I see. You and your brother, is it?"

"Yes."

He nodded casually. He wasn't sure where it was

he'd seen her face, or even whether he had seen it at all, but there was something about her that was ringing a bell.

"Nice part of the country, isn't it?" he said.

"Not particularly," said Tess. "I prefer the town, myself."

Garda Maloney was beginning to think that he was mistaken. This girl was far too relaxed to be in any sort of trouble. He smiled at her and she shrugged and lifted her eyes to heaven. "Family duty," she said.

The two neighbors were just closing the door of the potting shed. "Nothing there," said the sporty one.

"No," said Garda Maloney. "I think we'd better call it off. With any luck those goats are on their way back to wherever they came from. If they do turn up again you can let us know, and we'll have another try in the morning."

He accompanied Tess back to the front of the house. The other two men started up the path, and before he joined them Garda Maloney said, "Give my regards to your aunt." Tess looked heavenward again and ducked in through the doorway.

Kevin and Lizzie were sitting in the fireside chairs. Lizzie was eating stew out of a jelly mold and Kevin was eating his out of a small, dented saucepan with a bent handle.

"We left the dish for you," said Lizzie, pointing to the warming shelf beside the fireplace.

"Never mind that," said Tess, looking angrily at Kevin. "That was a great bit of thinking, that was, Mr. Rat, Mr. Streetwise, Mr. Hedgehog Brain!" Kevin stared at her in amazement.

"What are you talking about?"

"I'm talking about you, looking after Number One. You don't like cops, oh, no. What about me, then?"

"Children!" said Lizzie. "Stop squabbling! Where's your manners?"

"Oh, shut up about manners, Lizzie," snapped Tess. "And we're not children. This has nothing to do with you. I'm talking to this selfish little swine."

Kevin was growing darker by the minute, like a heavy cloud waiting to burst. "I don't know what she's talking about," he said.

"I'm talking about the garda! I'm talking about missing persons, descriptions, photographs. I'm talking about being on their records!"

Kevin swore. Lizzie looked as if she might object, but changed her mind.

"You should have thought of that, Kevin," said Tess. "I don't think like you do. I wasn't brought up to. It's your job to think of things like that!"

"And who do you think you are? Telling me what my job is!" He glared at her with such contempt that her anger evaporated and left a dull ache in the pit of her stomach.

"Come on now, girls and boys," said Lizzie. "Stop arguing and eat your dinner while it's hot."

Kevin poked around the dented saucepan with his spoon. "Did he recognize you?" he asked, sulkily.

"I'm not sure. I think he did, but I might have put him off the scent," said Tess.

"Not to worry," said Lizzie. "No sense in getting edgy, is there?" She handed Tess her stew in the dish they had saved for her. Tess looked at it gloomily. It had DOG written on the side.

chapter thirteen

Lizzie refused to let Tess and Kevin help her wash up, even though they really meant it when they offered. So they sat beside the fire and watched the flames licking around the kettle as she clattered around behind them.

"Funny thing," said Tess, emerging from her own thoughts, "but I can still feel the place where Long Nose bit off my tail. Ridiculous, isn't it, when I haven't even got a tail?"

"Like a phantom limb, I suppose," said Kevin. "You were lucky it was only your tail, though. If it had been your hand or your nose or something you'd be in a bit of a mess now, wouldn't you?"

"What do you mean?"

"Didn't you realize? If you get injured it doesn't just go away."

Tess had often noticed that scratches and bruises she got as an animal stayed with her when she switched back to herself. But it had never occurred to her that something more serious could be transferred from one form to another.

Kevin was unlacing his shoe. "You probably didn't notice but I have only three toes on this foot. Once, when I was a rat, I got the other two stuck in a crack in a drainpipe. There was no way to get out except to just keep pulling."

"Yeucch!" said Tess.

Kevin took off his sock. It was dark and stiff with dirt, and Tess was about to say something about it when she saw his foot. The last two toes, the smallest ones, were missing. It was slightly grotesque. "Doesn't matter what I am," he said. "If it has toes, those two are missing."

Kevin had started rubbing at the dirt between his remaining toes. "Put it away, will you?" she said. "It's disgusting."

He shrugged and pulled his sock back on. Behind them, Lizzie closed a cupboard door with an emphatic bang.

Tess leaned back in her chair and closed her eyes. She was suddenly very tired.

"Tess?" said Kevin.

"Yes?"

He was looking at her carefully and his concern was evident in his face. Here was yet another Kevin, one that she hadn't seen before now. But how did she know if she could trust him?

"Are you all right?" he said.

"I'm just tired. I don't really know what's going on."

"Maybe we should just hear what Lizzie has to say," said Kevin, "and then we can decide what to do. You can go home after that, if you want to. What do you say?"

Tess nodded and sighed, and settled more comfortably into her chair. As if in approval of her decision, a tabby cat hopped lightly up beside her and curled itself up on her lap.

Back at garda headquarters, John Maloney carried his dinner tray over to a free table in the cafeteria. His mind was littered with images of goats that did improbable things, and he couldn't shut them out, no matter what he did. As he began to eat, he spotted Oliver Griffin leaving the cashier with his tray. Maloney looked away quickly, but he knew he had been seen and that Griffin was coming to join him. In a crisis Oliver was about the finest person he had ever worked with because nothing, not even the most tense of situations, could deprive him of his sense of the ridiculous. There were times when John had found knots in his stomach being dissolved by unexpected laughter thanks to Oliver's sense of humor. But in the normal run of things, Oliver's eternal quipping was intolerable.

"Tough day, eh?" he said now, as he unloaded his tray. This was his breakfast. He had just arrived for the night shift. "Job getting your goat?"

"Don't start, Olly," said John. "I'm not in the mood."

"Ah, come on. It can't be that bad. Bit of sport for a change. Headline news. Big game hunting in Tibradden, County Dublin."

"I wouldn't care if I never saw another goat in my life. If you'd had to deal with them you wouldn't be laughing."

"Want to bet?"

John laughed despite himself and felt a lot better. "The worst of it was," he said, "the little beggars seemed to be enjoying themselves. You'd swear they were making fun of us."

"Probably were," said Griffin. "And I hear you had an encounter with the Lady of the Manor."

"Who?"

"Old Lizzie."

"Oh, her. Do you know her, then? Some character, eh?"

"Yes. Sitting on a fortune and still living like a gypsy."

"A fortune? What makes you think that?"

"All that land. All those fields around there. They all belong to her. About eighty acres, I think. Imagine what that's worth."

"Phew" said John.

Oliver finished his dessert and went on to his main course. John had seen how Olly ate enough times now not to be surprised, but it still made him feel slightly queasy. "Yes," Oliver said. "The developers are hovering around her like flies, but she won't sell. 'I has all I needs,'" he mimicked, "'and I needs all I has.'"

The accuracy of the imitation had John laughing again. "You must have been trying to buy the place yourself."

"Nah. I've known Lizzie for years. She's a great old character, really. There's more to her than meets the eye."

"I suppose so." John put down his knife and fork and started peeling an orange, trying not to look at the red puddles of ketchup on his friend's plate.

"Besides," Oliver went on, "I feel sorry for her in a way, with all the land speculators waiting around for her to die. Imagine thinking that the only thing the world wants from you is your death, eh? I'll be sorry when she snuffs it, but I'll get a great laugh out of it, too. Can you imagine the faces of those real estate dudes when they find out she's left everything to a home for retired donkeys?"

"Donkeys?"

"Well, she probably will, you know. Or goats. That'd be a good one."

John smiled despite himself. "She couldn't do that, though," he said. "Her relatives would be entitled to collect, wouldn't they?"

"What relatives? Lizzie hasn't got any relatives."

"Yes, she has. I met her niece today, or her great-niece, or something."

Oliver was shaking his head with a certainty that infuriated John. "Nope," he said. "Not Lizzie's you didn't. She told me herself that she has no one left in England and she never had a family in Ireland. 'I's all alone in the world and I likes it that way. I's no time at all for people, I hasn't. They takes up too much space.'"

"Well, you're wrong this time, Olly. I . . ." John stopped abruptly. The gentle tapping of suspicion that he'd had when he first saw Tess had become a mighty hammering. "Drink your tea, Olly," he said as he stood up.

"Why? Where are you going?"

"We're going, Olly. Missing Persons."

*     *     *

"I knowed it was going to happen," said Lizzie. "I knowed it as soon as I read about it in the newspaper."

Kevin looked across at Tess and raised a quizzical eyebrow. Tess shrugged.

"I gets the papers from Mr. Quigley. That's the farmer who owns those cattle. He gives me his old ones to light the fire."

Tess stroked the cat on her lap. She was relaxed now that she was almost sure she would be going home soon. She didn't know what she would say to her parents when she got there, but she would think about that later.

"Sometimes I looks at the papers before I scrunches them up," Lizzie went on, "and sometimes I doesn't. I always knows that if something's important it'll catch my eye. How can something be important if you has to go looking for it, that's what I says. So I wasn't surprised when I saw it."

"Saw what?" said Kevin.

"About that drilling up there in the North Pole. I knew that they would wake up the krools if they started drilling. But people never thinks about what might happen. They wants oil and they wants money and cars, and as soon as they's got them what does they do but want more of them? So I said to myself, I'll warn them. That's what I'll do."

She got up a little stiffly. The night had fallen so she drew the curtains, and for a while the room was soft with firelight. Lizzie rummaged around in a drawer until she found what she was looking for, then turned on the light and came back to her seat.

"There," she said, handing a piece of brown paper to Kevin. "That's only a copy, mind. I always keeps a copy of letters."

Tess leaned across and read the letter over Kevin's shoulder. It had been written in fountain pen and the illegible scrawl was accompanied by a great number of smudges and blotches. Tess knew without a doubt where that letter would have ended its life, and she wondered how many similar letters from cranks passed through government offices in the course of a year. She sighed and sat back. The cat made a tour of her lap and resettled itself.

"Well?" said Lizzie. "What does you think?"

"I'm sure it's a good letter, Lizzie," said Tess. "But the trouble is, people don't . . . I mean people in government don't very often take much notice of letters."

"Whoever they're from," Kevin added.

"You's right, there," said Lizzie, "and you knows why that is, doesn't you?"

"Why?"

"Because they thinks they knows it all, that's why."

Tess's face was among the first that John Maloney saw in the files on missing persons. "There she is!" he said to Oliver Griffin. "That's Lizzie's niece."

"But Lizzie hasn't got a niece," said Oliver.

"I believe you, Olly," said John. "*Now* let's go."

"People in general," said Lizzie, "thinks they knows it all. And if they doesn't know it then they puts it in front of a microscope or a periscope and makes it bigger, and there's things in this world should be left the same size they always was and not interfered with at all."

Tess looked at her watch. She would be home before her parents went to bed.

"They doesn't use plain common sense," Lizzie went on. "They sees things that is plain and simple and they goes to great lengths to make them as difficult and complicated as they can. They sees that the world is cold at both ends so they comes up with a cock-and-bull story about how we's all spinning around in the air like a football. But you can throw a football around all day and it never gets colder at the ends than it is in the middle."

"I don't think it's the spinning that causes the poles to be cold, Lizzie," said Kevin. "I think it's the way the earth tilts."

"Tilts?" said Lizzie.

"Yes. The earth is sort of leaning as it goes around, so some parts don't get as much sun as others."

"And where did you find that out?"

"I read about it in the library," said Kevin.

Lizzie got up angrily, spilling two cats onto the floor. "That's exactly what I's talking about," she said. "What does a nice boy like you want to go poking around libraries for? Nosing out all kinds of nonsense you has no use for? Then when you gets a chance of learning what you needs to know, there's no room left in your head for it." She strode over to the fire. "And you get a move on!" she said to the kettle, giving it a poke.

"Why don't you tell us anyway, Lizzie?" said Tess. "About your krools?"

"My krools?" said Lizzie. "They isn't my krools. They isn't anybody's krools. They's just krools."

"Well, tell us about them anyway, will you?"

"We's too far south to know about them here, that's all. They knows about them in Finland and Norwiegerland, and they knows about them in Siberia, except they has a different name for them.

They's big, cold, flat things like jellyfishes, and they sleeps in their own ice just like the grizzly bear sleeps in his own fat. They sleeps for thousands and thousands of years and while they's sleeping they doesn't bother the rest of the world. But if they gets woken up they gets hungry, and off they goes across the world, filling theirselves up again."

Tess glanced at Kevin, hoping to share a silent joke, but he was gazing solemnly into the fire.

"What about the other cold places, Lizzie?" he said. "Like the Alps and the Himalayas."

"Those mountains, you mean? But they's cold because they's high up in the sky. Everyone knows that!"

There was a long silence. Tess moved her chair a bit closer to the fire. Outside the wind was rising. Tess could hear the hinged cat entryway on the outside door rattling. At last, Lizzie sighed and shook her head sadly. "You doesn't believe me," she said. "I was afraid you wouldn't."

Tess and Kevin said nothing, because there was nothing they could say. From time to time, the wind made the chimney give a great pull which sucked flames up to hug the kettle.

"You doesn't believe in krools," said Lizzie, "and I suppose you doesn't believe in them dinosaurs, either."

"But dinosaurs are different," said Tess. "There's evidence for the dinosaurs. You can still see their bones."

"We doesn't know what it was left them bones behind," said Lizzie, "and krools has no bones to leave in any case. But if those dinosaurs was there, where are they now?"

Kevin was becoming irritable. "Everyone knows that, Lizzie. They became extinct."

"And does everyone know what happened to make them extinct?" asked Lizzie.

"There was a shift in the earth's crust and something changed in the atmosphere. That's what happened," said Kevin.

"There was earthquakes," said Lizzie, "and they woke up the krools, that's what happened. And the krools was hungry when they woke up, that's what happened. And the krools ate up all the dinosaurs that wasn't already dead and buried. That, you know-it-alls, is what happened."

Tess felt a shiver run up her spine. It was the kind of shiver she sometimes got when she read a good poem or heard a piece of music that touched on some deep and delicate truth that everyday language didn't reach. There was another long silence, and then Lizzie said, "It's snowing. I can smell it."

\*     \*     \*

The two policemen parked their car some distance from the top of Lizzie's path. Before they got out, they emptied all the loose change from their pockets and put it in the glove compartment. Oliver took the car key off its ring and left the others under the seat. There must be nothing that would clink or jangle. They intended their approach to be silent.

Lizzie's kettle was starting to sing. This time she knew where the milk was and the teapot was ready but even so there was plenty for her to bustle with. "Switchers isn't what they used to be," she said. "There was things we knew in the old days that you doesn't even begin to know."

"But what could we do, Lizzie?" said Tess. "Even if we did . . . I mean, even if it was true about the krools?"

"It is true," said Lizzie.

"Even if it is," Tess repeated. "What could Kevin and I do about it?"

Lizzie thought for a moment, swirling hot water around the teapot. "I doesn't know exactly," she said. "I's been thinking about it a lot, and I doesn't know exactly. But I knows this. Switchers has powers that you hasn't even dreamed about. You hasn't even begun to know what you can do."

"What do you mean?" said Kevin, suddenly interested.

Lizzie emptied the hot water into the sink. "I knows all the kinds of animals you two has been. And I knows that you hasn't done half the things I did when I was your age. You hasn't a notion of how much you can do."

"What can we do, Lizzie?" asked Kevin.

"Even I doesn't know that. If I had my time all over again I would try to find out. We all thinks we has all the time in the world when we's young. And sometimes we doesn't push ourselves hard enough. We doesn't use our imagination, so we never really gets to the bottom of ourselves. Sometimes we doesn't know what we could be until it's too late."

Kevin was listening intently, but Tess's mind was beginning to wander. Lizzie sounded too much like her parents and teachers, sounding off about how young people didn't make the most of themselves.

She looked at her watch again. She would have time for tea before she left, she decided. While she was drinking it she could try and work out a way to arrange another meeting with Kevin. She didn't want to go home without being sure that she was going to see him again.

Lizzie poured water onto the tea leaves.

And then came the knock at the door.

chapter fourteen

"Lizzie?" called Oliver from the front door. "Don't worry. It's only me, Garda Griffin." He knocked again.

"All right, all right," said Lizzie, making her way through the hall. "I's coming." She turned on the outside light, opened the door, and peered shrewishly at Oliver. "What does you want at this hour? Scaring old ladies in the middle of the night. You ought to be ashamed of yourself."

Oliver stepped past her into the hall and went ahead of her into the kitchen.

"Sorry, Lizzie," he said. "But this time it's not about goats. It's those two youngsters we're looking for. The ones who were here earlier."

"Why? What's they done?"

Oliver didn't answer, but went through the scullery and into the back porch, where he opened the door for John.

"What's he doing there?" asked Lizzie. "What's going on? Why can't he use the front door like everyone else?"

"We're just being careful," said Oliver. "In case anyone slipped out the back."

"Who's going to slip out the back? What's you talking about?" asked Lizzie.

"I don't think they're here," said Oliver to John. "But you'd better take a look upstairs, just in case."

"No, he won't," said Lizzie indignantly. "And don't you talk over my head as if I wasn't there! I's smaller than you is, but I's older than the two of you put together and you has no right to barge into my house as if you owned the place."

Oliver sighed. "I'm sorry, Lizzie. You're right. It's just that the young girl has run away from home and her parents are very worried about her."

"Oh, dear," said Lizzie. "And I thought they was such a nice pair of youngsters. Is you sure it was her?"

"Positive," said John.

"Then they told me a pack of lies. I always says you can never trust them teenagers."

"How long have they been gone?" said Oliver.

"Let me see, now. They left just after this young man was here looking for the goats, I think."

"But maybe you're expecting them back?" said John.

"No. Why should I?"

"Well, I was just wondering why you have three cups set out on the table."

There they were, three odd cups and three odd saucers with a jug of milk and a bowl of sugar beside them.

"Three cups," said Lizzie. "They's observant, isn't they, pussums, eh? Still, I suppose they has to be. That's what they's trained for. But maybe they's too clever, eh? Maybe there's things about an old woman's life that they didn't ought to ask?"

John felt a slight chill and looked around the room. The little old house was creepy at night, even with the lights on. He hadn't enjoyed the dark walk down the lane one bit.

"We have to ask, I'm afraid, Lizzie," said Oliver. "That's our job."

"They has to ask, pussums. But maybe they'd prefer if they didn't know?" Lizzie went over to the table and poured a drop of milk into each of the three cups. "I does this every night before I goes to bed. And in the morning, when I gets up, I does it again." She poured the tea and spooned in sugar. Then she put one of the cups in front of her and one to each side. "This one's for me," she said, "and this one's for my husband, George, who went off over the sea to fight in the war and never came home. And this one here is for our little daughter, Kitty, who died before she was even born."

John shuffled his feet in embarrassment. The cottage had suddenly become saturated with an appalling sense of loneliness. Even Oliver was silent.

"So," said Lizzie, brightly, "up you goes and take a look around upstairs. Go on with you."

"That's all right, Lizzie," said Oliver. "It won't be necessary."

"Indeed it will," said Lizzie. "You has a job to do and you's required to do it. And I has a reputation to protect. I won't let anyone have cause for doubt in case they says, 'Maybe she was hiding those two young criminals all along.' Go on. Up you goes."

The two policemen obeyed, sheepishly, and thumped up the narrow stairs. They stayed there only long enough to look around the doors of the two small bedrooms; then they came down again.

"Sorry about all this, Lizzie," said Oliver. "We didn't mean to disturb you."

"You's more disturbed than I is by the looks of things," said Lizzie. "Why don't you sit yourselves down and drink these cups of tea now they're poured?"

John blanched, and even Oliver's cast-iron stomach became momentarily queasy. "It's very kind of you," he said, "but I think we should move on." He reached down and picked up a ginger tomcat who had been asleep in Lizzie's chair. "I see you have a new cat?"

"I has two new cats," said Lizzie. "So you needn't be minding about me and my little habits. I has all the company I needs."

Oliver put the cat down and led the way to the front door. "Good night, Lizzie."

"Good night," she replied. The two men lit their flashlights and were soon hidden from sight by the blizzard. Lizzie closed the door and went back to the kitchen, passing on her way the army parka and down jacket that were hanging among her coats in the hall. "That was a close shave, pussums," she said. But she got no response, not even a glance. Every one of the six cats in the room was sound asleep. Lizzie looked at the three cups on the table. For a moment the loneliness still lying in the air closed in and settled on her heart.

Tess woke shortly before dawn. The fire had died down during the night and the room had become chilly. She yawned, then stood up and stretched, reaching out as far as her paws would go and catching them on the upholstery of the chair to check that her claws were sharp.

The other cats had gone on an inspection of the

night and not yet returned. Someone was sitting in a chair pulled up close to the fireplace, and Tess slipped down onto the floor, hoping to find a lap and get warm. But halfway there her other mind woke up, and she realized that it was Kevin.

She switched, feeling rather glad that she hadn't made it as far as his knee before she realized. He jumped slightly as she appeared, then nodded briefly and returned his attention to the fire.

A few dry logs had been propped up in the embers, but they hadn't been there long enough to light. Kevin was leaning forward with his elbows on his knees and it was clear that he was deep in thought. Tess pulled up another chair and spread her hands above the grate. "Cold," she said.

Kevin stirred and sighed but said nothing.

"I fell asleep," said Tess. "Cats are great, aren't they? There's nothing to beat a cat for comfort. I sometimes think that if I had to choose, I'd choose a cat."

Still Kevin said nothing, but went on gazing into the fire. Small flames began to catch the base of the logs and creep up their sides. Behind them one of the cats came in through the scullery door, but went out again when she realized that neither of them was Lizzie.

At last, he stood up and went over to the window. He pulled back the curtain and looked out into the darkness. Snowflakes were falling gently against the glass and little drifts had formed against the bottom of each pane. "I don't mind if you go home, Tess," he said. He let the curtain fall and came back to sit by the fire. "I'd probably do the same thing if I were you.

"But I have decided. I'm going up there. To the Arctic."

Tess stared, wide-eyed. "What? To look for Lizzie's krools? It's crazy, Kevin, it's a laugh. You really believe they're up there? Giant slugs that cause ice ages?"

Kevin shrugged. "I don't know."

"Well, I do," said Tess. "Lizzie's not so bad when you get to know her, but she's not all there. You saw that letter. She's harmless, but she's mad."

"And what about us, Tess? What would people call us if we told them what we do? What we are?"

"We don't tell them though, do we?"

"Of course not," said Kevin. "But why? What if you were to tell your parents where you've been for the last few days? What would they say?"

"They'd probably say I'd fallen in with a bad crowd and taken some funny drugs," said Tess.

"They might," said Kevin. "But I'd say the chances

are they'd take you to see a psychiatrist if you insisted on sticking to the truth."

"That's different," said Tess.

"We know the truth, and if worse came to worst we'd be able to prove it. But this business about krools is ridiculous."

Kevin said nothing. The fire was burning brightly now and sending out sparks onto the hearth. Tess got up and filled the kettle at the sink. Outside in the trees the first birds were beginning to complain about the weather.

"Besides," she said as she hung the kettle on its hook, "even if there really were krools, which there aren't, what could we do? You and me?"

Kevin leaned back in his chair. "That's the whole point, Tess," he said. "That's why I'm going. I'm as doubtful about this krool business as you are. I wouldn't be going, either, if it hadn't been for what Lizzie said about . . ." He paused. "What was it that she said, exactly? Something about not knowing what we could do. Not knowing half of what we can do."

"But we know that anyway, Kevin. Or I do, anyway. We're living in Ireland, you know? We can't go around the place being elephants and kangaroos and flamingos, can we? It'd be ridiculous."

"I don't think that's what Lizzie was talking about," said Kevin.

"What was she talking about, then?" asked Tess.

"I don't know. But when she said that we didn't know what we could do, I had the strangest feeling. I can't really explain it, but it was as if I knew for certain that she was right, and that there was all this strength and power in me that I didn't know how to use. I felt like I was filled with it, just waiting to explode, except that I didn't know how to set it off. There was nowhere for it to go."

Tess said nothing, not because she thought it was stupid, but because she was remembering times when she had felt like that herself.

"It's different for you," Kevin went on. "You still have a couple of years until you're fifteen. You can play around with this thing, you know? Experiment. Find out what you can and can't do. I don't have much time left."

The kettle came to life with a long, low moan. Tess gave in to her impulse to poke it. It swung slowly backward and forward for a while, but instead of singing louder, it went silent again.

"I want to go," Kevin went on. "Everything in me wants to go, even though I know there probably aren't any krools."

Tess sighed. "I don't think you're seeing things straight, Kevin. I mean, even if we . . . even if you did decide to go, how would you get there? All the animals are coming south, I've seen it on the news. It's impossible for anything to live up there."

"But that's the whole point!" Kevin leaned forward to look at her more directly, and his eyes were bright with excitement. "Don't you see? Because sometimes we don't know what we can do until we have to do it. And if we always stick with what's easy and safe, then we'll never find out what we're capable of. I want to know before it's too late."

Tess heard Lizzie's footsteps on the stairs. Somehow the cats did, too, because they came in from outside one at a time, shaking the snow from their paws.

"What's you two doing up so early?" said Lizzie.

"Just chatting," said Kevin.

Lizzie put her hand on her hip and used it as a lever to straighten her back. "Ooh. I's getting as stiff as a poker, so I is. All this cold weather doesn't do me any good." The cats purred and wound themselves around her ankles. She poked the kettle, which dribbled onto the fire but began, a bit reluctantly, to sing. "And has you come to any decisions with all that chat?" she went on. "Is you going to go sledding or play snowballs in the park?"

"I'm going north, Lizzie," said Kevin.

Lizzie straightened up as though she were twenty-one again. "I knew it," she said to the cats. "I told you, didn't I? He may not be all rat, I said, but he's got rat in him."

Kevin laughed, and suddenly Tess felt remote from them, as though she had been excluded. She realized then for the first time that if Kevin went alone up to the North Pole, she might never see him again. It was possible that he would come back and look her up, but what if he didn't? And what if it kept on snowing, and she and her parents became refugees and went south? How would he find her then?

"And what about you, Tessie?" said Lizzie. "What's you going to do?"

It hit Tess, then, with no warning, an expansive feeling that was so strong that it was hardly bearable. She was suddenly certain of her own strength and resourcefulness, and afraid of nothing.

"I, Lizzie," she said, "is going with him."

c h a p t e r   f i f t e e n

Lizzie made pancakes for breakfast, which Tess and Kevin ate much faster than she could cook. They drowned the pancakes in melted butter and syrup and ate them with their fingers. Nobody complained about the drips.

Tess was dreading the blizzards outside that she and Kevin would have to endure as they made their way north. She still had no idea how they were going to travel, and thoughts of her worried parents kept entering her mind, threatening to destroy her resolve.

As though she were reading Tess's mind, Lizzie said, "You thinks too much, girl. I's told you that before. And it's nothing but a waste of time. If you's finished with that pancake you better go over to the sink and wash your hands."

Tess got up and went over to the sink. Kevin followed. The water was icy cold and only hardened the butter on her fingers, but most of it came off on the towel. She handed it to Kevin and looked out of the window. The snow had already made little ledges of itself on top of every level spot it could find. Every branch, twig, and leaf bowed in submission beneath its weight. Tess could no longer remember the elated sense of power that she had felt before breakfast when she made the decision to go north with Kevin.

"Well? What's you waiting for?" said Lizzie. "Off you go, get your coats on. There's no sense in standing around."

Kevin went out into the hall and came back with their jackets. Tess put hers on, feeling like a small child who has been told to go out and play and has no choice in the matter. But it wasn't Lizzie, she knew, who was driving her to do it, or Kevin. It was her own pride. She was more afraid of disappointing herself than of losing their respect.

"Lizzie," said Kevin, "there's something I want to ask you before we go."

"Ask away," said Lizzie, pouring batter for her own pancake into the pan.

"You know what you were saying about the power that we have? How we can do things we don't even know about? Can you tell us about it? So that we know what kind of things we can do?"

Lizzie shook the skillet so that the pancake slid around. "I's been thinking about that," she said, "and I's decided that it isn't a good idea."

143

"But why?" said Tess.

"Because I doesn't want to put ideas into your heads. Because if I puts ideas into your heads they might turn out to be the wrong ones. And there's nothing that gets in the way of a right idea more easily than a wrong one."

"But can't you give us a clue, Lizzie?" said Kevin. "A couple of examples?"

"That's just what I doesn't want to do," said Lizzie. "I has no idea what you's going to find along your way and I has no idea how you's going to deal with it. But I does know this. I'd lock that door this minute and holler as loud and as long as I could for Oliver Griffin and his ignorant pal if I thought you was going to be in any danger that you couldn't manage. I knows that I could do it if I was still a Switcher, and I knows without any doubt that you can do it, too. So get on your way before you starts thinking about things, and be sure to call in and see me as soon as you gets home."

Kevin turned to Tess with a question in his eyes but she looked away and went toward the door. Her heart was numb with fear and she didn't want him to see it.

Lizzie came with them as far as the front step. "Good-bye, now," she said, as they walked out into the snow. "Look after yourselves. And don't be too busy concerning yourselves with what is. There's times when it makes more sense to think about what isn't."

Kevin turned to question her, but the door was closing in his face.

It was still early. Tess looked about her as they walked across Lizzie's front garden toward the narrow path. Apart from a few cat paw-prints, rapidly being filled in, there was not a mark on the snow. The birds were moving about in the trees and causing little avalanches among the branches, but they were not at all happy about the weather and saw no sense in going further afield before Lizzie came out to feed the chickens.

"What now?" said Tess.

Kevin shrugged. "Fly north, I suppose. There's no point in walking, is there?"

"Just like that?" said Tess. "Just fly north into a blizzard? Nothing worked out? No plans?"

"No plans," said Kevin. "No compass, no maps. And no hotels along the way, either, and no tents, no sleeping bags." Abruptly he gave Tess a friendly shove so that she stepped into a shallow drift. His nose was red from the snowflakes blowing into his face and he was grinning, so that Tess had the fleeting impression of a circus clown. "We're leaving everything behind," he said. "We're on our own. No rules, not even rat rules. Just the two of us, and all that out there."

All that out there was still filling Tess's heart with dread, but Kevin's eyes were shining. "Don't waste your fear, Tess. Save it up for when you need it, like the animals do."

She smiled, despite herself, and he smiled back, more openly than he ever had before.

"Pigeons?" he said.

Tess laughed, and they were friends beyond any shadow of a doubt, traveling with a common purpose. "I hate pigeons," she said. "Why not be something bigger and faster? We can be anything we want. No one's going to see us in this snow."

"Flamingos?"

"Eagles?"

"Swans?"

"Storks?"

"Albatrosses!"

"Yeah! Albatrosses." And two albatrosses were squeezing awkwardly through the hedge, running with clumsy strides across the wide meadow beyond, and finally rising with slow, graceful wing-beats into the white heart of the blizzard.

Without thinking, without even wondering how they knew, they tilted their wings and were heading north. They flew high, to avoid the hazards of tall buildings appearing out of the snow, and they stayed close together, one slightly beneath the other, so as not to lose sight of each other. Their powerful wings settled into an easy rhythm that they could have maintained for countless hours, but even so, it soon became apparent to them that they would have to choose some other means of travel. The snow was driving into their eyes and blinding them, and the winds were gusty and erratic and made it almost impossible to stay close together. On several occasions they lost sight of each other and had to circle and call until they met again. It was possible for them to continue as they were, but it would be a slow and anxious journey.

Dublin was beneath them. Most of the roofs were covered with snow, so the darkness of the more well-traveled streets stood out sharply. The traffic was quite heavy, despite the early hour, turning the shallow snow into slush. The two birds passed quickly over a sprawling area of housing developments, and were soon flying above the city center. There was no doubt about their destination. They were heading for the River Liffey.

As they came closer to the city center, and the buildings and traffic became more dense, Tess and Kevin could feel the slight rise in temperature. All those houses and offices were heated, and all the cars were burning fuel, and the excess heat was rising into the air. The snow seemed a little softer. It slid off their wings without sticking at all, and it didn't sting their eyes so badly. Surprisingly soon, the broad band of the river came into sight.

Tess was flying a little ahead of Kevin and below him, but he was constantly within her field of vision. All of a sudden, there was a wobble and a flutter of darkness where he had been, and then she was alone in the swirling snow. She wheeled in a great arc and turned back to see a black drake with a green head flapping toward her as fast as its little wings would carry it. Tess understood. Two albatrosses landing on the Liffey would undoubtedly cause more attention than they wanted.

The long spell of cold weather had caused parts of the river to freeze over, even before the snow had started to fall, but a channel through the middle had been kept clear by the current. If anyone had been watching, they wouldn't have been too surprised to see two ducks coming in to land and floating along downstream for a while. They would have been a little more surprised, however, to see both ducks dive, one after the other, and not come up again.

High above the polar ice cap, Lieutenant Harry Dodd was flying a medium-range bomber with a full complement of armed missiles. His copilot, Mark Anderson, was cleaning his fingernails with a tooth broken from a pocket comb. Harry Dodd hated Mark Anderson more than anyone on earth. As far as Harry was concerned, the only part of Anderson's brain that worked was the bit that handled the airplane. The rest of it was completely atrophied.

They were flying above the storm, in bright sunshine. Beneath them was nothing but unbroken cloud for mile after mile after mile. Harry's boredom was reaching critical levels.

"Anything on the radar, Jack?" he asked the technician. Jack's position was behind the two pilots in the body of the aircraft, where he was dozing over a bank of specially installed surveillance equipment. "Couple of planes," he said. "That's all."

"Theirs or ours?" There was no answer, so he said: "Ha ha. Theirs or ours. Joke."

There was still no answer. Anderson had finished cleaning his nails and was reading another of those dumb books that he seemed to go through like comics. Dodd had tried one once, but it made no sense at all. It was by some woman from Yorkshire who had been dead for a hundred years and whose brain, Harry was convinced, had been dead for a hundred and fifty.

"They think we're crazy, you know?" he said.

Anderson sighed and rested his book on his knee. "Who does, Doddy?"

"The ordinary people on the ground. They all think we're crazy.

"No, they don't," said Anderson.

"Yes, they do," said Harry. "And they're right, aren't they? We've got sixteen hundred U.N. planes in the air, day and night, dodging one another like a swarm of mosquitoes, and what are we fighting? A snowstorm."

"Don't worry about it, Doddy," said Anderson. "We're not doing anybody any harm. Let them think what they like." He picked up his book again.

"But I wasn't trained to not do anybody any harm!" said Dodd. "I wasn't trained to spend eight hours a day pretending to be a weather satellite!"

"Come on," said Anderson. "Look around you. The sun is shining in a clear blue sky. At least we're not down there wearing snow goggles and dodging polar bears."

"Anything would be better than this," said Dodd. "Sitting up here and getting bedsores on my rear end with some lunatic who reads . . . what do you call that stuff, anyway?"

"Literature," said Anderson.

"Literature! That isn't literature!" said Dodd. "Literature is what they give you when you can't decide which hi-fi system to buy. I've got piles of it at home."

Anderson wasn't listening. He was mentally absent again, reading his book.

"Anything new, Jack?" said Dodd.

"Couple of planes," said Jack.

# chapter sixteen

chapter sixteen

Goats had the secret of mischievous fun, it was true, but the spirit of pure joy had been perfected by another species and made its own. Two of these creatures were now speeding down the River Liffey, keeping well below the surface except when they had to rise briefly to catch air. They were dolphins, and they were heading for the open sea.

There are other sea creatures as fast as dolphins, but there are none that enjoy their speed so much. There are other sea creatures that live among their own kind, but there are none that take so much pleasure in another's company. And on land or sea, there are no creatures anywhere that get such enjoyment out of merely being alive.

As dolphins, Tess and Kevin sped down the River Liffey, catching the strongest currents to help them on their way. They stayed close together, weaving around bridge supports and making small detours to get a quick look at interesting bits of wreckage on the riverbed. There were baby carriages, bicycles, supermarket carts, there were sunken boats and cars, and once they passed a bus, with its rows of silted windows gazing vacantly toward the surface.

Tess knew that if she had to choose now, she would not be a cat. There was nothing that compared with being a dolphin. Her awareness was acute, her intuition sharp, and her body flowed with the current, all comfort and sinuous strength. If there had been time, she would have stood on her tail in the water and laughed at the people crossing O'Connell Bridge or walking to work beside the river. She would have done it not because she wanted their attention and applause, but because joy, more than anything else in the world, is for sharing.

Many, many miles away, between Norway and Iceland, the nearest krool was sliding toward them along the top of the rapidly expanding ice cap. It knew nothing of dolphins and nothing of joy. All it knew was cold and an endless, relentless hunger.

From above, the krools were invisible. They were round and shallow, roughly the shape of an upturned saucer, and so huge that they could cover an average-size town without leaving any trace of it. Because they were very much colder than the air around them, snow didn't melt when it landed on their backs, but gave them a coating of camouflage. So perfectly did they blend into the surrounding snowfields that they could not be seen at all, even when they were moving, except by someone unlucky enough to be in their path.

For krools will stop at nothing when the time comes around to expand their icy kingdom across the globe. They will slide over land or sea on the carpet of ice that they spread for hundreds of miles before them with their snowy breath, and as they travel they will eat anything of animal or vegetable origin which lies beneath the snow or above it. Trees, rocks, houses, and all the ice and snow that cover them are swept into the great maw of the krool and processed by its phenomenal digestive system. It sifts out what is useful and discards what is not as a powdery mixture of ground ice and stone. And the more it eats, the larger and colder it becomes.

The only enemy the krool fears is heat. The heat of the drilling rig had enraged the krool who encountered it, and caused it to heave and shudder for several days before it regained its strength and went on.

At the mouth of the River Liffey, Tess and Kevin turned east into the Irish Sea, then northward up the coast. They stayed close to the shore, where the water was warmer, but even so it soon became clear that they would need more insulation than they had, to cope with the cold seas ahead of them. There was only one possibility for a journey as long as the one they were about to undertake and, reluctant as they were to change out of dolphin form, they knew that they would have to.

The oceans, as any seaman will testify, exist in a different part of time from the land. If anyone were to ask Tess how long her journey through the Irish Sea and up into the Norwegian Straits took her, she would have been unable to answer. How long is an hour? An hour doing homework or an hour at the funfair or an hour when you're too sick to go out and play. How long is an hour for a whale? For the whole of that trip beneath the waves, time was a currency without value, as meaningless as money is to a frog.

Tess's human mind was all but engulfed by the phenomenal intelligence of the whale, and it was as much as she could do to keep her purpose intact. Whales have a knowledge of the whole global ocean with its varying currents and temperatures and moods, not as a person remembers someplace they have been, but as they might know their own house or garden without ever having to think about it. But more than that, they could know each part of their

155

immense home and what was happening there, even though they were not in it, for the voices of whales travel far and their thoughts travel farther.

This much Tess might have been able to remember, but it was only the tattered and tawdry edge of the truth, the way that words can only explain the edges of dreams and not their vivid depths. The whole of that world could not be held in the limited mind of a human being, and was lost to her forever when the time came to leave the oceans behind. But the thing that Tess never forgot was the whales' sense of honor. For the whales know the ways of the ocean from top to bottom and from end to end, and that means that they know where the whaling boats lie. It is not stupidity which makes whales easy prey for the harpoons, but their knowledge that the ocean is their own, and that it is better to die than to move even by the width of a flipper toward the fainthearted existence of the hunted.

Krools move with astonishing speed when they first wake up. The polar regions were territories that they had already claimed, even as they slept, and that needed only to be crossed. But the higher the temperature the harder they had to work to freeze the earth and the slower they moved. By the time they had reached the line of sixty-five degrees latitude, which runs through the middle of Norway and Sweden and through Siberia, Alaska, and northern Canada, they were already slowing down. Their snowstorms still preceded them by hundreds of miles, but would spread more slowly as they blew toward southern Europe and the U.S.

The krools on the Norwegian Sea were having a particularly hard time of it. They had long since passed the edge of permanent pack ice and were having to use enormous reserves of cold to freeze the surface of the sea before them as they went. It was a hungry time for them as well, because there was no nourishment to be had from the sea, whose citizens stayed well below the freezing surface. All krools are dangerous, but a hungry krool is the most dangerous of all.

When Tess and Kevin reached the fresh edge of the ice cap now lying between Iceland and Norway, they said good-bye to the world of the whales and turned themselves into seals for their reemergence onto land.

Despite their layer of blubber, they were shocked by the intensity of the cold. Snow was still falling, but it was a very different kind of snow from the large, soft flakes that were still settling on Dublin. Here the particles were small and dense, as though the air itself were ice that had lost its solidity but nothing of its coldness. It froze their whiskers as soon as they flopped out of the sea, and it stung their nostrils and eyes.

Tess stood beside Kevin, both of them blinking against the swirling snow and wondering what to do. Her mind searched for possibilities, but there were only two. To turn back, or to go on. It was Kevin who made the decision. He touched her nose briefly with his, and began to shuffle himself forward. Tess followed.

But seals are cumbersome on land, and unhappy. Their exertions warmed them but they were making little headway. After a while they stopped to rest, but as soon as they did, the cold began to bite into them again. So they moved on in a more effective manner, as polar bears this time.

Tess was torn between conflicting instincts. She wanted to turn back, to the solid safety of whales and dolphins and home, but at the same time she was afraid of being separated from Kevin in this white and terrifying world. She knew that nothing would persuade him to give up, even though she had long ago forgotten the feeling that had made her understand why. She had the awful sensation of being caught up in his life, his search for some intangible thing that she neither understood nor wanted. It made her feel help-less, with no choice but to trail along and accept what-ever was going to happen.

As far as she could see, there was only one thing that could happen. They would walk into the snow and ice until they could walk no longer, and then they would die. She shuddered and shook a crust of snow from her coat. Her fur was thick, but not thick enough, she knew, to protect her much longer.

Kevin was still walking with silent determination, but the snow was getting deeper and it was soft and powdery, which made progress slow and tiring. Tess's eyes and lungs were sore from the bitter air. She dropped her head. White bears, white snow, white air constantly moving around them. The only change in all that whiteness was when, from time to time, Kevin turned around to make sure she was there, and then she saw his black nose and eyes.

It was almost a relief when night began to fall. To Tess, numb with cold and exhaustion, it no longer seemed to matter what form rest might take, as long as it came soon.

Kevin stopped. In front of them was a miniature mountain, an iceberg that had been captured and imprisoned by the spread of the krools. Some of its facets were too sheer for snow to lodge there and the ice showed through, darkly opaque like crystal. To Tess it represented an obstacle, but to Kevin it was a godsend. Because around its base the snow had gathered into wide, deep drifts. He began to dig.

# chapter seventeen

chapter seventeen

In the middle of the night, Tess woke. It was absolutely dark in the snow hole. If any moonlight or starlight filtered through the clouds above, it failed to make its way through the tunnel they had dug and into their tiny cave.

It was surprisingly, luxuriously warm in there, from the trapped heat of their furry bodies. Tess would have stretched if there had been room, but they had made the space just big enough for the two of them to sleep curled up, so that they wouldn't have to warm any extra air. She yawned and turned over so that she was facing Kevin, and now she realized why she had woken. It was a long time since she and Kevin had talked together, and she wanted to do it now before daylight came and urged them into action. She switched, and immediately felt a little frightened to be lying in total darkness with a large bear. She could smell bear fur and bear breath, and before it frightened her any further, she reached out and tugged at Kevin's thick, warm coat.

He started, then grew rigid, and then the coat between her fingers was cotton, a little damp.

"You idiot, Tess! Don't ever do that again!"

"What? What did I do?"

"I was a bear, you fool. You woke me up. I nearly ripped out your throat!"

"Wow."

"I only just remembered in time."

"Sorry," said Tess.

Kevin said nothing, but turned awkwardly in the cramped space until he was on his back. Tess was afraid that she was going to cry, and as if he realized, he reached out his hand and touched her arm.

"It's okay," he said. "I shouldn't have shouted. I'm sorry."

Tess turned so that she was on her back as well and their shoulders were squeezed tight against each other in the dark. For a long time they lay in silence breathing the warm air.

Tess's mind was a jumble. She knew that the most sensible thing to do was to turn back and go home, but she couldn't say it to Kevin. It would seem like a betrayal after they had come so far. And if they weren't going to go back, what did you say to someone when it might be your last conversation with him? There was an awful sense of the executioner's cell about the snow hole. And despite all they had been through together, Kevin seemed like a stranger again, lost in his own thoughts. But it was he who spoke first.

"What did Lizzie mean, Tess, about what isn't?"

"I don't know," said Tess.

"But what could she have meant? It must have been important or she wouldn't have said it," said Kevin.

"I don't know if that's necessarily true," said Tess. "Lizzie said an awful lot of things that weren't important."

"Oh, come on, Tess. You're not going to start talking about backing out again, are you? It's hardly time for that, you know."

"Maybe it is the time for it," said Tess. "Maybe it's the only time. The last chance we have." She expected Kevin to be angry, but his answer was surprisingly calm.

"No, it's too late for that now. We've come this far because we believed what Lizzie said. It'd be completely pointless to give up now, just when we're getting to the heart of it."

"The heart of what?" asked Tess.

Kevin shrugged, and they were squeezed so tightly together that Tess's shoulder rose with his. At another time she would have laughed, but at that moment laughter seemed to belong to a different life.

"Of what we are, I suppose," said Kevin. "Of survival, of freedom, of independence." He sighed. "But I don't know what the problem is. My mind feels as if it's shot through with steel cables or something. Whenever I try to think about anything a bit different, like what isn't, I just find myself running along the same old lines. I can't seem to get anywhere."

"I suppose we haven't done too badly so far" said Tess, "and most of the things we've done have been your ideas. The dolphins and the seals and the polar bears and this hole in the snow."

"Yes. But it's all practical stuff, isn't it? It's all what is and not what isn't. We can't go much farther as polar bears, can we? And we can't hole up here forever, either. We need something else now. Some leap of imagination."

He fell silent again. Tess closed her eyes, and must have dozed for a moment because Kevin's voice woke her from a dream.

"Have you got your watch on?" he asked.

For some reason the dream was important, but when she tried to remember it, it slipped away from her. It was all snow, anyway, ancient and endless. She felt her wrist. "Yes."

"Has it got the date on it?"

Tess was already looking at it. "It says seven-thirty," she said, "but I suppose the time is different up here. I can't see the date. It isn't luminous. Why do you want to know, anyway?"

"I was just wondering when my birthday was. It must be quite soon."

"What date is it?"

"The thirtieth. Can't be that far off now."

Suddenly Tess realized why he was asking. She had an awful image of Kevin losing the ability to change and being stuck out there in the frozen wastes. He would freeze in no time in that stupid parka. He didn't even have gloves. And going back would be just as dangerous. He might be in the middle of the sea when it happened, or up in the air. It was important to know.

"Haven't you got a match?" she said.

"Good thinking," said Kevin, fumbling in his pocket.

The first match he struck hurt their eyes so much that they couldn't see the watch. As the second one was burning down, Tess held the watch up close to it.

"The twenty-eighth," she said.

Just before the flame died, she caught the look of dismay in Kevin's face. Their situation seemed even more hopeless than before, if that was possible. But Kevin said, "Never mind."

"Never mind?"

"I was just thinking we might have had a bit of a party, that's all. But we'll have to skip it."

"A party? Are you out of your mind?"

"No. It's part of the tradition, apparently. The girl who told me about it had one. I didn't really know her very well. She wasn't like you. But she invited me to her party, and I went. The day before her fifteenth birthday."

"Why the day before?"

Kevin laughed. "You can't very well throw a party if you're an eagle, can you?"

"An eagle?"

"Yes. She was into discos and motorbikes and stuff. An eagle suited her actually. It was her kind of thing."

"You mean . . . You mean you can choose?"

"Of course!" said Kevin. "Didn't you know that? Whatever you are at the time of your birthday, that's what you stay. You can't switch anymore, that's all. But there's nothing to say you have to be human."

Tess stared into the darkness, trying to absorb this new information.

"I've spent months worrying about it," Kevin went on. "Ironic, isn't it? Months trying to choose between a rat and a sparrow hawk and an otter, and now it looks as if I won't have a choice at all. I'll just have to take whatever I get.

"No, Kevin," said Tess. "We could still get back."

"I don't see how we could," said Kevin. "But in any case, I am not too worried about it. I can't understand it, really, but ever since Lizzie said what she did, about us having more power than we know, I've had this kind of faith. I'm not worried about those things anymore. They don't seem to matter."

"But you can't just end up as a polar bear or a walrus! You're human, Kevin, you have to be human!"

Kevin laughed, and Tess felt her heart fill with despair.

"Why?" he said.

But she couldn't tell him. She couldn't explain that she wanted to dress him up and take him to a French restaurant, or that she would welcome him any time she got off the bus after school and found him waiting. Even if her pride would allow her to say these things to him, it made no sense out here with the arctic gales blowing all around them.

"I never was any good at being human," Kevin said. "Even with my family, even before I knew what I was. I don't know why. I just didn't have the knack. My brother did. He was older than me, and he got along okay with everyone. My father's a toolmaker. He makes all kinds of bits and pieces that people want. My brother was always out in his workshop with him, helping him. But I couldn't take an interest in it. I always got everything wrong, no matter how hard I tried."

"So what?" said Tess. "That doesn't mean anything."

"It did, though. It meant that I didn't fit in with the men in the family, you see. And my mother . . ." He stopped for a moment, and then he went on. "I don't know quite how to explain it. She was always there, always. She never had a job, she never went anywhere, she was there every day when I came home from school and she did all the things that mothers are supposed to do. But in another way she wasn't there at all. She wasn't there for me. Her mind was always on something else, on what she was doing or on what she was listening to on the radio, or on something that she kept locked away inside herself somewhere."

Tess noticed that the snow cave wasn't as warm as it had been. The cold seemed to be creeping into her from below, and she turned onto her side to relieve the discomfort in her back.

"When I look at it now," Kevin went on, "I see that she just didn't have it, that thing, whatever it is, that attention that people give to each other. I don't blame her for it. But at the time I used to think it was my fault, that I just wasn't good enough to be worth bothering with."

It was very quiet in the cave. Kevin cleared his throat and went on. "But then I got angry about it, and it worked, because at least when I was bad she took some notice of me. That was around the time I discovered I could turn into a rat. It was ages before I discovered that I could be other things as well. In those days I used to set off for school in the mornings and spend the day with the other young rats.

"Even when my parents knew I was skipping school, there was nothing they could do to stop me. If they took me to school in the morning, I'd slip off somewhere at break. The other kids hated me because I was different, and I hated them because they weren't."

"I know the feeling," said Tess.

"Yes. And as time went by I stopped bothering to go home. When I did turn up from time to time, they used to get upset and talk about reform schools, so I thought it was best to just stay out of the way."

"Did you never spend time being human then, after that?"

"Oh, yes. I still turned up for their birthdays and Christmas, things like that. After a while they just accepted my absence and stopped asking questions. And I told you I spend, spent, a lot of time in libraries. Sometimes I'd meet someone on the way and hang around with them for a while. But I never had a real friend. Not until . . ."

"Until what?"

"Phew. It's getting cold in here, isn't it?"

"Yes. We're not as warm as the bears were. What were you going to say just now?"

"It doesn't matter."

Tess rested her head on the crook of her elbow. She was colder than she had realized, and beginning to feel drowsy again. She knew that it was dangerous. She remembered reading about how the cold sends you off to sleep, and then you never wake up.

For a while Tess resisted sleep and listened to Kevin's steady breathing in the darkness. What if they both fell asleep here? No one would ever find them. If the weather changed and the ice melted, their bodies would slide into the sea and be lost forever. The thought of all those fathoms of dark water beneath them filled her with horror, but also a strange sort of resignation. They were so small in the middle of all this air, water, and ice. There was nothing else for hundreds of miles. Suddenly, she could not find any more resistance. She allowed her mind to drift away and there was a deep, deep sense of comfort.

The forgotten scene from her earlier dream returned. It was a landscape as bitter as the one outside their snow hole, but there was something moving across it, some kind of animal. And suddenly, Tess was wide awake.

"Kevin!"

He jumped at the urgency in her voice and she knew that he, too, had been asleep. "What?"

"I've got it! All that stuff about what isn't. It's so simple, I can't believe we didn't think of it before." Tess sat up so that the top of her head was wedged against the roof of the snow cave. "Lizzie was right. We're completely caught up in the things around us, just trying to copy what already exists. But what about something that used to exist, and doesn't anymore?"

Kevin was holding his breath, and Tess could feel his sense of excitement. "Go on," he said.

"Well, what about when there really was an ice age? There were animals that lived in those times, weren't there?"

"What, like dinosaurs?"

"Yes. Except that the dinosaurs didn't make it. They didn't adapt. But some other creatures did."

Kevin let out his breath with a gasp. "Mammoths!" he said.

171

"Exactly! I saw them, Kevin, just now in a sort of dream. Walking through the snow. And why shouldn't we be mammoths? We know what they looked like. I'm positive we could get a feel for them."

"Of course we could. It'd be a lot easier than being a whale."

There was no more to be said and they fell silent, their minds full of new hope. After a while, Tess said, "We ought to be bears again, Kevin. Until the morning. It's too cold in here. It's dangerous."

"Yes, you're right," he said, but he didn't switch, and Tess had a feeling that he was waiting for something. "Don't go to sleep again," she said.

"No. I'm not. I was just thinking about getting stuck as a mammoth if my birthday came."

Tess said nothing, and Kevin went on, "I know there's nothing you could do about it. I wouldn't ask you to stay with me or anything. But maybe you could . . . I don't know, just keep an eye on me somehow. So I wouldn't be completely alone."

"Of course I would, Kevin. I'd do anything. I'd go to the ends of the earth if I had to."

"I know you would," he said, and then he laughed. "You already have, in a way, haven't you?"

Tess's pride reared up. "I didn't come here just because of you, you know," she said.

"I know that," said Kevin. "But you're still the only friend I ever had."

Before she could answer he was a bear again, and with a sigh she joined him.

# chapter eighteen

chapter eighteen

The two mammoths moved slowly but solidly across the snowfields. Their shaggy eyebrows and whiskery nostrils protected them from the effects of the freezing air and their long, woolly coats provided perfect insulation against the blizzard. So little heat escaped through their coats that snow landing on their backs didn't melt, and even provided a further layer of protection. It also provided a partial shield against the sensitive infrared scanners in the planes that passed from time to time above their heads.

Harry Dodd was flying his plane low through the white heart of the blizzard.

"Anything new, Jack?" he asked over his shoulder.

"Nah," Jack mumbled.

There was little or no danger of encountering anything in the air. The high points in the pack ice were well charted, and their radar screens would give warning well in advance of anything that might be in their path. Even so, Harry found it nerve-wracking to be flying so totally blind.

"That freighter out of the way?" he asked.

"Hell," said Jack, "that was an hour ago. He'll be over Stockholm by now. Wait a minute, though."

Even Anderson put down his book for a moment.

"Nothing," said Jack. "Infrared's just picking up a couple of animals down below. Small ones. I don't know how they can survive down there."

"Poor beggars," said Anderson.

"Poor beggars?" said Harry. "They're poor beggars? What about us?"

The only danger that the mammoths were aware of was hunger. There was no source of food for miles around, not even the rough arctic vegetation on which they had learned to survive in the past. Their reserves of fat would keep them going for a while, but for how long they didn't know. It took a lot of energy to keep those massive bodies warm, and a lot more to keep them moving.

But keep moving they did. Tess and Kevin had passed another test. Kevin's faith had held, even if Tess's hadn't, and circumstances had proved him right. The mammoths were slow but they were comfortable, and they were making steady progress toward the north.

The hours passed. The human parts of their minds chafed at the tedium of the changeless landscape, but mammoths had learned patience over the generations, and they plodded along tirelessly.

Long before they were able to see it, the krool sensed them coming. Its small, uncomplicated brain went into a momentary seizure. Although it was a poor thinker, its memory was as long and as ancient as its life, and it was well acquainted with mammoths. The prospect of encountering these two was not a pleasant one.

A dead mammoth is an agreeable snack for a krool, but a live one is a different proposition entirely. This particular krool had once had the experience of swallowing a whale that had been trapped beneath the ice, unable to breath and dying. Its phenomenal internal temperature had crippled the krool, and it had never forgotten the agonizing days that followed as it battled with the heat from the whale the way a person battles with infection. Even two live mammoths would not be as bad as a whale, but they would nevertheless create a considerable disturbance in its digestive system, and it would have to rest for a while until they were absorbed.

In the normal course of events, a krool would not even consider eating a mammoth, and when it encountered one it would flatten the leading edge of its mantle. The mammoth wouldn't know it was there and would traverse the krool's back until, after a few hours, it reached the other side. If the particular krool Tess and Kevin were approaching had not been so hungry, it would have allowed the two mammoths to go their ways. But it could not allow any source of food to escape, even if it caused a bellyache. It lay still and waited.

Some miles away, Harry Dodd's bomber had completed an in-flight refueling operation and started its return journey. In a few more hours it would make a radio-controlled landing on the salted runway of an air base in central England, and its crew would get out of their air-bound prison.

Jack was dozing. Anderson was reading. Harry, determined to defeat boredom, was flying as low as he dared.

Tess and Kevin blundered straight into the waiting krool. One moment there was nothing ahead of them except untrodden snow. The next moment a whole section of the snow lifted and towered above them. They were gazing with horror at the black underbelly of the krool. For an instant, Tess thought that the world had collapsed and she was staring into nothingness, a gaping abyss. Then she saw the eye. A single, huge, unblinking eye, gelid and green, looking straight at her.

If Lizzie had been wrong, it would have been the end, not only of the two mammoths, but of Tess and Kevin as well. For the mantle was above them now and the huge, cavernous maw was opening as the krool pushed forward to swallow its prey. But if Lizzie had been wrong she would not have sent the two young Switchers out to test their strength against the krools. Lizzie knew, and quicker than thought, Tess knew, too, that they did indeed have powers beyond their wildest dreams.

Kevin had been right. If they hadn't been faced with the ultimate test of their skills, they might never have learned them. Because, if there had been time for thought, Tess would never have believed that what happened next was possible. The krool's mantle was dropping like a monstrous flyswatter. Not even a bird would have had the speed to dodge out from under it. But Tess switched, quicker than she had ever switched before, and suddenly the krool was rearing away again and backing off.

For Tess's heart had understood even more clearly than her mind what Lizzie had meant by being what isn't. And it had acted before her mind had been able to doubt, and to stop it. In front of the krool's retreating underbelly was a huge and magnificent dragon, and then there were two of them, blasting flame at the hideous eye, which shriveled and melted and dripped like warm syrup into the snow. The krool reared as high as it could go, a mile into the sky, but the dragons took to the wing and continued their pursuit until it collapsed and doubled back on itself like a monstrous black pancake.

The two dragons leaped for the skies in a delirium of delight. They were faster, cleverer, more powerful than any creature on earth, and they swooped and soared, chased each other's tails and tumbled in the air in sheer elation. This was the feeling that their premonitions had promised them, the certainty of power beyond human imagination, the sensation of absolute freedom. For all the elements were theirs to enjoy. They were equally at home in water, earth, and air, but they were not bound by any of them. They carried the secret of fire within them, and even the great ice wastes all around them could cause them no discomfort. They were the rulers of all they surveyed, and there was no creature on earth that could defeat them.

In the midst of their celebrations, a plane passed

above them in the clouds. They heard it first, then saw it with their infrared vision.

At the same time it saw them. The scanner beeped, warning of a strong signal. Jack sat bolt upright and stared at the screen.

"Have you got something, Jack?" said Harry.

"Good God," said Jack. "What the hell is that?"

"What is it, Jack, what is it? Have you got something?" Anderson sat up and turned around in his seat.

"I've never seen anything like it," said Jack, his eyes filled with wonder.

"What on earth is it, Jack?" Harry yelled.

Jack moved into military mode, sharp and efficient. "We have hot spots, boys. Two of them. I don't know what they are and I don't know where they came from, but they're not like anything I've ever seen before."

Anderson had left his seat and was standing in the small space beside Jack, looking over his shoulder at the screen. "Swing around, Harry," he said. "We're losing them."

"Who's giving the orders around here?" screamed Harry. "What the hell are you doing standing back there telling me what to do?"

"You should see this, sir," said Jack. "We should get a better look before we go past."

Harry gritted his teeth and swore, but he dipped his wings and swung around in the tightest circle the plane could handle. "Come in, base," he said into the radio mike. "This is Delta Zero Five, are you reading me?"

General Rupert Heyford-Hunt, chief coordinator of the U.N. Arctic Task Force, was snoozing at his desk in Mission Control when one of his technical assistants called him over to the computer terminal. "Good Lord," he said when he saw the pictures Jack had transmitted. "What on earth is that?"

"Damned if I know," said the aide. "There's no plane in the world that flies like that."

The shapes on the screen were descending in rapid circles, leaving a residue of heat in their wake that showed up on the monitor like the tail of a comet. The plane was passing above them and moving away again.

"Get onto the boys in that plane," said Heyford-Hunt. "Tell them to stay above those things and keep sending back pictures."

chapter nineteen

As dragons, Tess and Kevin were not easily intimidated by the plane flying above their heads. They agreed to ignore it and go in search of more krools. One went East and the other West, flying low enough to be able to see the ground beneath them.

The plane followed Kevin. After a while he grew irritated by it, doubled back on himself, and then flew south at top speed.

In the plane Harry Dodd swore. Jack shook his head. Mark Anderson went back to his seat and his book.

A krool in a snowstorm is not easy to find. Even for a dragon. Kevin scanned the ground as he flew, but it was only by chance that he came across his second krool. It was sliding southward across Norway, more slowly now than in the preceding weeks, but still making good progress. It had fed well recently, cutting a great swathe through the forested regions in its path, and had grown to enormous dimensions. Krools do not reproduce like most of the other creatures of the earth. They don't mate with others of their kind, and they produce neither eggs nor young. When they reach a certain size, however, they divide, simply split down the middle and become two, like amoebas. Kevin was able to spot this krool from the air because it was beginning to do just that.

Where it was splitting into two the camouflage of snow was shifting and revealing patches of the glutinous black flesh beneath. Kevin slowed, wheeled around, and returned, spitting flames. But by the time he reached the krool, it had become aware of the hot little presence above and glued itself firmly to the ground.

The first krool had been so easy to dispose of that Kevin wasn't prepared for the battle that followed. The krool below him now did nothing, merely sat tight, knowing that as long as it didn't reveal its underneath to the attacker it was almost invulnerable. Almost, but not quite. Kevin came in time after time, throwing flames constantly. Wherever he attacked the krool, it melted into black oily liquid, but it was so huge that his best efforts made little impression on its bulk.

He stopped for a while, trying to work out a plan. It was tiring, the way he was acting, and he realized that he was using too much energy. If he became exhausted he would have to rest, and then feed, and when he thought about feeding his mind became filled with pictures of what dragons best like to eat, which is people. And when he thought of people, he could think only of people that he knew, and he wondered if any Switchers before him had experienced the weird sensation of imagining a meal consisting of their relatives and friends.

To take his mind off these unpleasant thoughts, he returned to the krool and flew up the gradual contour of its body until he reached its highest point. Then he directed flames at one spot, calmly and consistently, until he had produced a hollow like a cauldron full of bubbling black liquid. At last the heat melted a hole right through the krool and the liquid flowed away onto the ground beneath it. The beast began to convulse, heaving its great body so that the snow that covered it flew up in a thick cloud. Kevin hovered in the air and waited until the krool gave a final shudder and lay still.

High above, a satellite had picked up the heat emissions from the battle, and three planes were converging on the spot where Kevin and the krool had fought. But by the time the planes arrived Kevin was gone, and their surveillance equipment picked up no signs of life.

A few hundred miles away, above Greenland, another plane was about to intercept Tess's path. Her infrared image had just appeared on the aircraft's monitor, and a radio communication from Mission Control had put the crew onto the offensive. Heyford-Hunt didn't know what those things were out there, but he wasn't taking any chances. The first heat-seeking missile was armed and ready to go.

Tess's flight path was erratic and unpredictable, but as soon as the pilot of the bomber got a clear radar fix, he fired off the missile and swung around out of the area.

Tess had known that the plane was nearby, but she hadn't realized that she could be detected. She knew that as a dragon, she could see objects by the heat they emitted, but she had no idea that there was an equivalent technology available. So, when she picked up the image of the missile snaking toward her, she was caught completely off guard. If she had been expecting it, she might have dodged, since dragons can perform fantastic aerial maneuvers that no missile could possibly follow. Instead, instinctively, she switched and changed herself into a swallow. The missile swept past, catching her in its current of air and swirling her around in the blizzard. Then, finding itself without a target, it ploughed blindly on, straight into the snow beneath.

The swallow was well clear of the center of the explosion, but even so, chunks of snow and ice flew up to where she was recovering her balance high above. She flew upward and away, but in no time at all the blood of the little bird began to freeze. She listened for a moment, and as soon as she was sure that the plane was not returning she switched back into the warm and fearless form of the dragon.

The monitor in Mission Control slowly cleared and became blank as the heat from the explosion died away. A great cheer went up. General Heyford-Hunt leaned back in his chair and clasped his hands behind his head in satisfaction. "Whatever it was, we got it," he said.

"Uh-oh," said a technician behind him. "I'm afraid not, sir."

"What?" Heyford-Hunt sat up again. There, on the screen, was the hot spot, as clear as ever. It was heading east with surprising speed. "But it disappeared, didn't it?" asked Heyford-Hunt.

"It looked as if it did," said the technician. "Maybe the heat from the explosion just masked it somehow. It's there now, anyway."

It was, racing through the snowstorms toward Kevin. He had heard her call and was flying toward her. From their positions all over the arctic circle, the military planes moved in.

\*    \*    \*

It was nearly dark when the two dragons met above
the Norwegian Sea, and it was time to call it a day.
Their infrared vision enabled them to see planes overhead, but no kind of vision would enable them to find
krools in the dark. Kevin wanted to remain a dragon
for the night, but Tess had learned that they were not
as invisible as they had believed, and insisted on the
safety of polar bears. Kevin capitulated. They dug in
quickly and went to sleep immediately, curled closely
together for comfort.

As soon as the sun came up the next morning, the two
hot spots were picked up on the monitors of a surveillance plane. They didn't appear gradually, as a
plane does when it starts its engines and warms up,
and they neither taxied to a runway nor rose verti-
cally. One moment there was nothing on the infrared
screens, and then there were two large, hot objects
flying off at impossible speed in different directions.

This time, Tess and Kevin had a plan. It was a dangerous plan and would require all their courage and all
their wits but, if it worked, it would get rid of the
krools. All they had to do was find them.

They had decided to fly low, so low that a krool
would appear to them as a patch of slowly rising

187

ground that would then fall away again. In the middle of a blizzard such flying required steel nerves and lightning fast reactions, but the dragon has both, even at the speed of a jet plane.

When they had talked in the early hours of the morning, Tess and Kevin had agreed that there must be a large number of krools along the same latitude as the first ones they had found, to account for the even progress of the blizzards that preceded them. So the dragons flew in straight lines, due east and due west.

Several times, Tess slowed and circled to examine a suspicious slope in the ground, but each time it was a false alarm. Above her the planes crisscrossed continuously, and she had already avoided three missiles before she found her first krool.

As soon as she was certain it was a krool on the ground, she rose into the clouds above it and circled steadily, waiting. Before long she saw the telltale heat of the approaching plane and heard its engine. As soon as it was within range, it launched its missile. Tess dived at full speed toward the unsuspecting krool. The missile spun after her, coming closer to her tail, until at the last minute she switched as she had done before and swung out of the way.

It worked. The momentum of the dragon dive

flung the little bird out into the blizzard at terrifying speed, and away from the explosion. A few bits of exploded krool reached her as she shot through the air, but she was too busy trying to gain control of her dizzying flight to be concerned about them.

At Mission Control, the observers watched the clearing screen in tense silence. Then someone said, "We got one this time."

There was no cheer. This had happened before. "Don't count your chickens," said Heyford-Hunt, then groaned as the hot spot reappeared and resumed its eastward flight.

On the other side of Greenland, heading west, Kevin was playing the same game, with slightly more success. He had discovered a better way of finding his prey.

A krool crossing land leaves a distinct trail behind it where it has cut a mile-wide path through the vegetation and left nothing but a clean sweep of powdered snow, ice and rock. Kevin happened to notice this when he found his first krool of the day, and after that he stopped looking for their convex forms and searched instead for abrupt tree lines or abnormally smooth stretches of snow. The method served him well. He found krool after krool, and each time he hovered above them and waited until the military arrived with their heat-seeking missiles.

As the day wore on, General Heyford-Hunt grew increasingly exasperated. The events of the day were beginning to send shivers down his spine. It was becoming clearer all the time that whatever those things were, they were playing games with him. The phone was ringing from the media office a little too often and the questions were becoming embarrassing. But the strangest thing of all was that whatever was happening out there was having the desired effect on the weather. Already the blizzards were dying out and the clouds were disappearing from large areas that had previously been covered. In southern England and Ireland, he was told, the sun was shining and the snow was beginning to melt.

It was just in time for Lizzie. For the first few days of the blizzards, Mr. Quigley had been extremely helpful. He had come every day with supplies, and he and his daughter had shoveled the snow away from her door and made paths to Nancy's shed and the henhouse. Then, one day, he had told her that he had sold all his stock and managed to get a passage for himself and his family on a ferry to Cyprus. He could not let the opportunity pass. He brought Lizzie provisions for a fortnight and a hundredweight of rock salt to help against the snow, but beyond that he could do nothing.

When the daily digging became too much for her, Lizzie brought Nancy and the hens into the house and let them have the use of the laundry room. The plumbing had long since frozen tight, so Lizzie had filled the bath and the sink and a few old milk churns with snow. Then she brought in as many logs as she could stack in the hall and closed the doors. She was dug in like an Arctic creature in her little snow hole of a cottage, and was forgotten by the world. The drifts rose until they covered the downstairs windows, and since the power lines were down over half the country Lizzie moved around in the dim light of the fire, saving her candles for emergencies.

The oats Lizzie fed to Nancy and the chickens ran out and she had to start sharing her own rations with them. Then water began to get scarce. The plug in the bath had proved useless, and the snow that Lizzie had gathered so laboriously drained away as soon as it melted. She was reduced to scraping snow from the drifts outside the windows and melting it over the fire. By the time the sun appeared, Lizzie was exhausted, dispirited, and almost down to the last of her provisions.

If it hadn't been for the cats, she would probably not have known that the snow had stopped. With the windows all covered in drifts the kitchen was dark, but it was too cold to sit upstairs where there was light. The cats, however, went up and down quite often during the day to use the litter box that Lizzie had set up in the spare room for them as soon as they could no longer get out.

When Moppet failed to return from one of these visits, Lizzie went upstairs to investigate. She found him curled up on the windowsill in the sunshine. For the first time since Tess and Kevin had left her house, Lizzie's stiff old back straightened up. She went to the window, pried it open, and called out to the sky, "You did it, you little horrors! You made it!"

# chapter twenty

chapter twenty

At the edge of the arctic circle the dragons were still at work. Tess and Kevin had discovered that dragons can communicate over great distances, and they kept each other informed of their progress. As soon as Tess learned Kevin's method of detection, she began to attack the krools on her side of the planet. Before long, their numbers were dropping dramatically.

In Mission Control, General Heyford-Hunt was tired of ordering missiles to be launched at infrared ghosts. He had found some pilots who volunteered for close combat in fighter planes armed with machine guns and close-range missiles, but they had flown back bewildered. As soon as they came anywhere near to visual range, they reported their targets disappeared. Simply vanished without a trace.

With outward confidence and inward despair, Heyford-Hunt continued with the missile attacks.

Tess and Kevin were in a mood of high exhilaration. They were living by the skin of their teeth, dodging death one minute and tempting it the next. As a result, life had never seemed better or more precious.

And they were winning. Their phenomenal speed had taken them around the globe to meet again above Canada. They played aerial tag and leapfrog together for a few minutes before separating and starting back, one circling east, the other west, picking off the krools they had missed.

Heyford-Hunt followed their progress on radar and infrared. He now knew that he was playing into their hands in some way, but he also knew that the snowstorms were abating. He didn't know how he was going to explain it, but he was sure of one thing. He was going to take all the credit when the time came.

The one in the west was circling again. "Let him have it," he said.

Fast as the dragons were, they couldn't make it back around the globe before nightfall. They could call to each other, though, and they did, before they came to land and settled as polar bears into their separate dugouts for the night.

Tess slept fitfully, dreaming bear dreams and dragon dreams, and terrible dreams of Kevin trapped in the form of some awful creature for the rest of his life. A single bear produces very much less heat than two curled up together, and she woke before dawn stiff and sore with the cold. She knew that the only way to get warm was to get moving, so she crawled out of the tunnel and was amazed to find herself standing in the middle of clearly visible snowfields, stretching away in all directions, glowing in the light of the stars that shone out of a cloudless sky. A plane passed low over her head, blinking a single white light. Tess shook her damp coat and began to trot northward.

At Mission Control, General Heyford-Hunt was drinking his fifteenth mug of coffee. The meteorological satellites were beaming down gratifying pictures of the cloud formations. A few isolated blizzards were still stretching southward like thick fingers, but otherwise the area below the line of seventy degrees latitude was clear.

But Heyford-Hunt knew that the hot spots, whatever they were, would return in the daylight. He had spent most of the night in a fury of injured pride, and he wasn't about to admit that they had won. There were all kinds of theories buzzing around. Some officers speculated that the hot spots were Iraqi war machines, developed for the purpose of freezing out the Northern Hemisphere and crippling the American and European economies. Others said they were UFOs making a bid to colonize the planet. Heyford-Hunt was willing to believe that they came from outer space, but nothing that had happened had succeeded in convincing him that they were not living beings of some kind. He hadn't forgotten those two tapes.

As Tess made her way north, she warmed up and began to make plans. The blizzards had died down because the krools were dead, but there would surely be others closer to the pole that would need her attention. She was reluctant to become a dragon now that the cover of clouds had gone, just in case some low-flying plane might get a sight of her in the starlight. So she switched instead to a Canada goose, and began to fly steadily north.

She was right about the krools. What she didn't know, however, was that they were no longer a danger. They were under increasing threat from their greatest enemy, the sun. Only in large numbers can krools be certain of producing sufficient freezing clouds to keep covered and safe. A single krool cloud can be dispersed by warm winds and leave its maker helpless, melting in the sun. Already the second and third line of krools were in rapid retreat, and the rear guard had retraced their tracks and slithered back into their icy beds.

Kevin woke at dawn, and the first thing that occurred to him was that it was the day before his birthday. He had one more day and one more night before he had to make his enormous decision.

He emerged from his den and stretched. It was still snowing, but the snow was softer than it had been. He was feeling fresh, and ready for another day's action, but first he wanted to have a look around, and he knew exactly how he was going to do it. In the blink of an eye he was a dragon again, moving rapidly up toward the top of the clouds.

The air force was waiting for him, and a passing plane let off a missile as he rose toward it, but he switched and dodged it easily. It exploded beneath him, not far from his snow hole. When he recovered his equilibrium, he became a dragon again and set off at high speed toward the North Pole. He flew so fast that he soon outdistanced the planes behind him, and by doubling and zigzagging as he went, he was able to confuse the controllers on the ground until at last he found that he had a clear sky above him. Rapidly, he dropped a couple of hundred feet so that he could give himself the momentum he needed, then he launched himself like a rocket, straight up through the clouds and into the air above them.

It was similar to the way a spaniel will jump up above the long grass to get a look around, except that Kevin went up almost as far as the stratosphere. From there he could clearly see the pattern of clouds beneath, which told him the exact locations of the outlying krools. It took him scarcely a second to learn what he needed to know, and then he was dropping again, like a monstrous hawk plummeting down through the sky.

In front of the monitors at Mission Control, a dozen mouths dropped open in disbelief as radar relayed Kevin's astonishing feat.

"What on earth," said General Heyford-Hunt, "are we dealing with?"

Just across the Arctic Circle from Kevin, Tess had reached the safety of clouds and felt she could switch unseen. She could hear Kevin calling, giving her the whereabouts of the krools, and the two dragons set about finishing them off.

It was easy now. All they had to do was to sweep down along cloud formations until they found the krools. After a while, Mission Control began to understand the pattern, and quite often the dragons found that the planes were already in position even before they arrived.

By late afternoon, Tess and Kevin had located every

krool that lay outside the line of seventy degrees latitude. They met directly above the North Pole, where
night had already fallen, to celebrate and discuss tactics.
Kevin was full of the joys of victory and was in favor of
carrying on, but Tess wanted to stop and talk to him.
For a while they argued in the air, until they became
angry and began to burn each other's noses and ears
with jets of flame, which sobered them up a bit.

In the end, Kevin relented and they sprinted away
from the planes that were gathering above them. Then
they switched and became geese, and flew on until
they came to a strange amphitheater of ice in the middle of the Greenland Sea. As soon as they landed they
returned to their human form.

"Phew," said Kevin, when they stood face-to-face
at last. "It's cold."

"Yes," said Tess. "So we have to talk fast."

"What's so important, anyway?"

"This," said Tess. "We've got the krools on the run,
right?"

"Well, we've knocked most of them out, anyway."

"Right. And I knocked out two today up in northern Greenland that were definitely going backward.
So listen. Maybe the job is finished, you know? And
even if it isn't, I could always finish it off on my own
if I had to."

"But why should you?" asked Kevin.

"Because maybe you can still have the chance to be what you want to be," said Tess.

"But there's not much choice up here is there?" asked Kevin. "Anyway, I quite like being a dragon."

So did Tess, but if she had been a dragon at that moment, she would have burned his nose again. "Don't be an idiot, Kevin," she said. "We've only survived so far because we can switch! If you couldn't dodge those missiles and become a polar bear at night you wouldn't stand a chance!"

Kevin sighed. "I suppose you're right," he said.

"But this way you still have a chance," said Tess. "With the speed we can travel as dragons, we could be in Ireland before morning. We might even have time for a birthday party. At Lizzie's maybe?"

"It's a bit risky, isn't it?" asked Kevin. "They'll be able to follow us on radar, won't they?"

"So what?" said Tess. "We've been dodging planes and missiles for two days, now. What could they possibly throw at us that we couldn't handle?"

Kevin said nothing. Tess rubbed her gloved hands together and blew on them. "Come on, Kevin," she said. "It's too cold to stand around and think about it."

"I suppose it is," said Kevin. "The only problem is, I still don't really know what I want to be. There was something nice about not having to choose, you know?"

"But you don't have to choose right now," said Tess. "You'll have tonight to think about it. And in any case, you'll probably know what to choose when the time comes, won't you? The same way you knew it was right to come up here?"

Kevin brightened. "You know something?" he said. "For once in your life, you might be right."

# chapter twenty-one

chapter twenty-one

General Heyford-Hunt was on the edge of his seat. "Come on, my tricky little friends," he said to the moving blips on the monitor in front of him. "You just keep right on going the way you are."

The two UFOs were heading south, right out in the open above the Norwegian Sea. He had been following their progress for some time, watching the satellite pictures with growing anticipation. If they carried on in their present direction, they would soon be crossing the northwest tip of Scotland. And when they did, he would have a little surprise waiting for them.

At an air base in North Wales, Harry Dodd and his team were getting ready for takeoff. They were in a line of planes crawling toward the runway, waiting their turn. The snow was still thick on the fields all around, but the skies were clear.

Harry was eager for action. "Know something?" he said.

"Not a thing," said Anderson, who was carefully checking over the instruments on the panel in front of him.

"I have a feeling we're going to see some action tonight," said Harry. "It's in my bones, you know? After all, we were the first to spot those two aliens out there, weren't we?"

"I haven't seen any aliens," said Andersen.

"What were they, then?" asked Harry. "They weren't planes. Everyone knows those two things weren't planes. You'd have to be a nutcase to think those two things were planes."

"Nobody knows what they are," said Anderson, "and nobody knows how to stop them. But I don't see any point in talking about flying saucers and getting ourselves all worked up."

"All worked up?" said Harry. He jammed on the brakes as he came up onto the tail of the plane in front, and the three of them lurched forward into their seat belts. "Who's getting all worked up? I'm not getting all worked up. Are you getting all worked up? Nobody gets all worked up in this bird, not as long as I'm in command."

Anderson sighed and continued with his last-minute checklist.

"All I'm saying," Harry went on, "Is that we were

the first to see those two aliens, and I have a feeling we're going to be the last."

"Did you see any aliens, Jack?" said Anderson.

"Couple of planes," he replied.

There were no missiles aboard the bombers that lifted off, one after another into the starlit sky. They were fully loaded though, but this time with another kind of weapon.

When Harry and his crew took off, Tess and Kevin were still well out over the Norwegian Sea. They were flying low, skimming close to the waves, enjoying their flight. The night air was clear and fresh, and they were beginning to believe that they had finally left the battlefield behind.

Once they had passed over the line of new ice that the krools had made, they got an occasional glimpse of a whale breaking the surface of the sea. They knew that they were heading away from the cold, toward life again.

Tess looked across at Kevin flying beside her, and it seemed that it was the first time she had been able to relax for days. What they had done was impossible. It made no sense at all, and yet it was true and they had done it. The starlight shimmered off the metalic scales of Kevin's back as he turned to her and winked.

She was a dragon flying with another dragon across the sea beneath the stars, and she took time to drink it in and fix the images and sensations into her mind. Because she knew that whatever else happened, she would never feel like this again.

Within an hour, the thirty-five planes had reached their positions and were set in a holding pattern, waiting.

"Do you have a reading on them yet, Jack?" said Harry.

"Only what the satellite's sending."

"Are they far off?" asked Harry.

"About fifteen minutes, I should think." said Jack.

"What's that on the radar, then?"

"Let's see," Jack paused. FT6R. That's Pete and Hank coming around again. Hi, guys."

"Hank," Harry spat. "That's what you get for working with this international crowd. Whoever heard of a serviceman called Hank, for God's sake. Must be an American. With a name like that he should be riding rodeo horses, not fighting in a war!"

"I'm not sure this is a war, Harry," said Anderson.

"Read your book, Anderson. That's what some people do. Some people are born to read books and some are born to fight wars. I don't care what anyone else says, but when I'm in a plane, I'm fighting a war."

Anderson broke one of the last spines from his comb and picked his teeth with it. "You can say that again," he said.

As the north tip of Scotland came into view, the two dragons did a quick loop-the-loop of delight. Heyford-Hunt, along with fifteen assembled advisers and assistants, held his breath. When the two UFOs resumed their course the printouts on his table fluttered in the breeze.

The dragons were over land now, with the ragged western coast of Scotland to their right. Beneath them, the trees of huge forestry plantations poked their dark heads above the snow. Occasionally the sharp eyes of the dragons could make out the roofs of abandoned villages and isolated farmhouses. Tess was surprised to find that now and then she got a whiff of wood smoke. There were people still surviving somehow, despite the depth of the snow. She was looking down, trying to get a glimpse of the heat of hearth fires, and Kevin must have been as well, otherwise they would have not been taken so utterly by surprise by finding themselves flying straight into the path of an oncoming plane.

"They're going to pass right under us!" yelled Jack.

"And we're going to get them," said Harry.

"Okay," said Anderson. "Just take it easy, now. Are we all clear of other planes, Jack?"

"All clear. And we're on computer countdown, seven, six . . ."

"Damn, where are they? They don't have any lights or anything."

"Four, three . . ."

The dragons were practically beneath the plane before they had time to blink.

"Two . . ."

Tess acted goat, swung wildly to her left and upward, switching into a swallow as she did so.

"One . . ."

But Kevin was just bit slower. He flew straight on, and as he flew he switched.

"Zero!"

But he was too late. The napalm bomb dropped from the undercarriage of the plane and exploded in the air, scattering its flaming contents of sticky jelly through the sky and down to the forest below.

"We got them!" yelled Harry. "Did we get them, Jack, did we?"

"Get what?" said Anderson. "I didn't see anything. Did you see anything?"

"I didn't see anything, but I'm sure we got them,

whatever they were. Did we get them, Jack?"

"How should I know? I couldn't see anything."

"But you got the machines. What do the machines say?"

"The machines say there's a big fire behind us, that's all."

"Is there anything flying away from it?"

"Yeah. Us."

"I knew it," said Harry. "I could feel it in my bones. We got them."

Jack was still watching the satellite monitor in the back of the plane. "I wonder," he said.

"I'm certain of it," said Harry. "And do you know something else?"

"What?" said Anderson.

"This is going to be cause for a celebration. I'm going to buy you a brand-new comb."

By the time Tess got control of her flight and swung around to see what was happening, the plane was gone and the forest was blazing. Above it, she could just make out a speck of flame that twisted as it tumbled down and was lost in the thick smoke and sparks that rose from the inferno beneath. Her bird mind was utterly calm and detached, but her human mind was screaming, "Switch, Kevin, switch!"

But it would have been no use. Nothing, not even

a dragon, could have survived those flames. Kevin was done for.

Nonetheless she waited, an eagle hovering high above the forest as the fire reduced it to a skeleton of charred tree trunks and melted the snow around its edges. She stayed long after the planes had stopped circling and gone away. She stayed until the dawn arrived, the dawn of Kevin's fifteenth birthday, but all it brought was military helicopters coming to examine the aftermath of the fire. They would find nothing.

With a heavy heart, Tess wheeled and flew away.

chapter twenty-two

chapter twenty-two

Tired and dispirited, Tess made her way back to Dublin. It was a difficult journey. She tried being several different birds before she finally settled on the arctic tern. It was a tough little bird, she discovered, and coped well with the cold and the long hours on the wing. Even so, she was ready to drop by the time she spotted the Phoenix Park and came in to land.

In her house the lights were on. Tess stood among the trees across the street and looked around carefully. There was no one around. The snow was melting fast, but there were still deep drifts around the trunks of the trees and against hedges and walls. The prospect of warmth and rest was almost irresistible, but even as she made the switch, Tess realized that something was wrong. Much as she loved her parents and longed for the comfort of home, what she needed above all else at this moment was understanding.

The shock and grief she felt at Kevin's death struck her with full force now that she was human again, and it was something she would never be able to share

210

with her parents. There was only one person in the world that she could tell, and that was Lizzie.

Reluctantly, Tess turned her back on the bright lights of her parents' house and returned to the shape of the brave little seabird. On tired wings she crossed the city and searched among the snowy fields and trees for the ruin of the big house and the little cottage beside it. When, after some time, she found it, she was relieved to see smoke rising from the chimney and paths cleared to the sheds. She landed on the roof of the henhouse and looked around for a while before she decided on the best way of getting into Lizzie's house without alarming her.

The other cats arched their backs and hissed when they heard the stranger come in through the catflap and scratch at the kitchen door, but Lizzie knew straight away.

"You's back" she said as she opened the door. "That was quick!"

Tess switched, and the cats scattered into the corners of the room. Lizzie looked at her in concern. "You's worn out, girl. What's happened?"

Tess flopped, exhausted, into a chair. The seat had been warmed by the cats, and for a long time Tess sat in silence, letting the warmth sink into her and waiting for her strength to return. Lizzie set about making tea, but she did it quietly, and soon the cup was pressed gently into her hand. She sat up and sipped the sweet tea, but still she could not speak. "Rat-boy, huh?"

Tess looked up. A twitching brown nose was poking out of the fireplace hole, an unusually long nose. Tears began to pour down Tess's cheeks. Lizzie took off her slipper and threw it at the hole. Long Nose squeaked and disappeared, but a moment later he was back.

"Nanananana," he said. "Tail Short Seven Toes curled up with Long Nose and Nose Broken by a Mousetrap. Us guys sleeping. Sun rising, us guys bright eyes, hungry and strong."

Tess nodded through her tears. "He's right, Lizzie," she said. "You and I can talk in the morning."

"Off you go, then," said Lizzie. "But don't forget to come back to me, will you?"

"Of course not." Tess gulped down the last of the tea, then put down the cup and switched. As soon as she was a rat, she felt better. Rats live together closely, but without attachment or sentiment. As a rat Tess felt Kevin's death was an absence, but it was no longer a loss or a cause for grief. She shook herself and began to groom, to put herself back in order, but Lizzie picked her up and lifted her to the hole in the chimney before the cats could catch her. There she touched noses with the other rats, and quite dispassionately told them her adventures as she followed them through a twisting network of passages and underground tunnels.

Long Nose loved her story, and made her tell the part about meeting the first krool again and again, until eventually they arrived at their destination, a snug nest beneath the cowshed. Tess curled up close against Nose Broken by a Mousetrap. The last thing she heard before she fell asleep was the sound of Nancy, drowsily chewing her cud.

The next morning, Tess made her way back to the cottage. In human form again, she told Lizzie everything that had happened. The old woman listened carefully, slapping her knees with delight at each new development in the story. When Tess finished, they both sat quietly for a few minutes, then Lizzie said, "If I remembers right, you likes pancakes for breakfast."

Tess looked at her in astonishment. "How can you think about pancakes, Lizzie? Aren't you upset about Kevin?"

"No," said Lizzie. "I isn't. There are those who say there's life after death and those who say there isn't. But until I gets there myself, I isn't in any position to say one thing or another."

"But that isn't the point," said Tess. "I'm sad because I won't see him anymore."

"Then you's sad for yourself, girl, not for Kevin."

Tess looked into the fire. The flames were just taking hold of the wood, leaping up toward the kettle, sending sparks up to disappear into the darkness of the chimney. Lizzie got up and began to crack eggs into a bowl.

"Maybe you're right," said Tess. "I don't know. But the thing I can't understand is why it should have been us. I mean, why was I born a Switcher, and Kevin. And you, why you?"

"But all kids is Switchers," said Lizzie. "Didn't you know that?"

"What do you mean? How could all kids be Switchers?"

Lizzie began to beat flour into the eggs. "All kids is born with the ability. But very few learns that they has it. You has to learn before you's eight years old, because after that your mind is set and you takes on the same beliefs as everybody else. A lot of kids find out they can switch, but when their parents and friends say it's impossible, they believes them instead of theirselves. And then they forgets about it, like they forgets everything that doesn't fit in with what everyone else thinks. It's only a rare few who has enough

214

faith to know that they can do it no matter what the rest of the world thinks."

"So was it all just chance then? Just coincidence?" asked Tess.

Lizzie was beating furiously at her batter. "Chance?" she said. "Coincidence? I doesn't know what the words mean."

A movement in the chimney hole made Tess look up. One crooked nose and four small ones were poking out of the hole, and five pairs of eyes were fixed upon her. "Grandchildren," said Nose Broken by a Mousetrap. "Tail Short Seven Toes telling krools, mammoths, dragons, little ones watching."

The four small noses quivered in anticipation. Tess laughed, and while Lizzie fried the pancakes, she told her story once again.

Tess's parents had chosen not to escape the weather and flee to southern Europe. Instead they had stayed in the city hoping for Tess's return. When the snow began to melt and the roads were cleared their hopes rose, but by the time she finally knocked on the door they had almost given up on her. They greeted her with tears and laughter, and there was much talk of forgiveness and all being well that ends well.

But they found it difficult to adjust to the changes

in Tess. She had always been aloof, preferring her own company to that of others, but now it was more than that. She had become a stranger to her parents, and in all the years that followed they never learned more about her absence than they had heard from Garda Maloney's report. All they knew was that she had been away with a boy, and that she would not or could not discuss the matter. It was clear from her withdrawn behavior that in some way or other her journey had ended badly, and they believed that she would tell them about it in her own time.

So, although her parents noticed that from time to time Tess wore a silver ring that they had never seen before, they didn't ask her about it. They left her alone and tried to resume family life. Tess tried, too, but it was clear to all of them that she was acting mechanically and not from her heart.

Throughout her first weeks at home, Tess realized that although the date told her that it had not been so long since she left her bedroom window in the form of an owl, by another reckoning it was a year, a lifetime, an ice age. She could barely remember the child that she had been.

At school Tess made an effort and succeeded in finding one or two friends. Having friends helped to pass the time, but it did nothing to relieve the deep loneliness she felt, nor did her occasional trips to the park, to enjoy the company of squirrels or birds or deer for an hour or two. She was not a part of their world, she knew, nor was she a part of the world of home and school. She was somewhere in between, and all alone.

Her sense of isolation increased whenever she turned on the TV or radio and heard discussions about the famous "Northern Polar Crisis." The krools, as she suspected, had retreated back into the ice cap. They left no trace of their passing apart from the mysterious barren pathways which stretched for hundreds of miles through the vegetation in the arctic circle. A thousand theories were put forward, and it seemed that there was a new one aired every week. Each was as ludicrous as the last, but what really made Tess's blood boil was the unanimous agreement that Rupert Heyford-Hunt and Harry Dodd were the heroes of the day. And no human being apart from herself and Lizzie would ever know the truth.

Tess's parents never reproached her, but she knew that they had suffered a lot when she disappeared. They didn't try to stop her going for walks in the park. But they extracted two promises from her: never to be away for more than two hours and never to go out at night without telling them where she was going. Tess knew that in their terms these were reasonable requests and she agreed. She was sure that in time her parents would come to trust her again, and she would have more freedom. In the meantime she would have to live without seeing either Lizzie or her friends the rats.

So she had to look elsewhere for comfort. She saved up her pocket money until she had enough to buy the biggest cage in the pet shop and the nicest white rat they had. Her parents were surprised, because Tess had so often expressed her disapproval of keeping animals in captivity, but they didn't object.

The rat, however, turned out to be a terrible disappointment. It was terrified of the brown rat that Tess became when she switched, and it was terrified to leave its cage. When she did finally tempt it out into the room, it was timid and clumsy and slow, and no amount of persuasion would bring it to attempt the stairs.

The worst of it, though, was that the poor, stupid creature could not even speak Rat. It had been born and brought up in a cage like its parents and grandparents, and it had never been allowed, much less encouraged, to use its intelligence. It had a few basic word-images, but beyond that it was mute, and no effort on Tess's part succeeded in teaching it. The white rat was a mental infant, and would remain that way all its life.

He was company, nonetheless, and quite often Tess would lie awake at night, listening to him exercising on his wheel while she mulled over her experiences and thought about the decision that would face her in another year, when she turned fifteen.

Time after time Tess dreamed of the possibilities that awaited her, weighing the peaceful lives of dolphins and whales against the briefer but more thrilling lives of rats and goats. Time after time she seemed to reach a satisfactory decision, only to remind herself of how heartbroken her parents would be if she were to disappear from their lives forever. On a particular night a few days after the new year, she had just decided, once again, to stay human, when something happened that was to make her think all over again, in an entirely different way.

It was the white rat's sudden silence that alerted her to the change in the atmosphere. She watched him sniff the air, then turn around and gaze steadily into the darkness outside her window. As she got out of bed and crossed to the window to look out, the hairs on the back of Tess's neck prickled.

There, on the same tree that the owl had once called from, was the most beautiful bird Tess had ever seen. It was familiar to her, somehow, and yet she was sure that she had never seen it before, or any other like it. Its bright feathers glowed in the light cast out from her room, and its tail hung down below it, much longer than its body. Then, suddenly, Tess remembered the page of the book where she had seen the bird pictured, and even before she noticed that it had only three toes on its right foot she knew that it was Kevin. She knew that he had learned, in the nick of time, to find for himself the invisible path that lies between what is and what isn't. As he fell, burning, that autumn night that was the eve of his birthday, he had made his final, irreversible switch, and become the only creature, either of this world or not of it, that could survive that raging fire. And when the helicopters had left the following morning, he had appeared again, rising from his own ashes; a beautiful golden phoenix.

Tess's heart leaped, racing ahead of her into the night skies where she would soon be flying beside her friend. With a silent apology to her parents for breaking her promise, she reached for the latch and pushed open the window.